A FRIEND
A GOOD
IS LIKE
A BOOK
Ex Libris
I WOULD
FOREVER
KEEP
*S*UR*I*O*S*

Henrietta M Gunderson

THE

SEVEN VOYAGES

OF

SINDBAD THE SAILOR

THE

SEVEN VOYAGES

OF

SINDBAD THE SAILOR

Literally rendered from the Arabic into

French by J. C. Mardrus, and then translated

into modern English by E. Powys Mathers

with an introduction by C. S. Forester

and illustrations by Edward A. Wilson

New York : The Heritage Press

INTRODUCTION

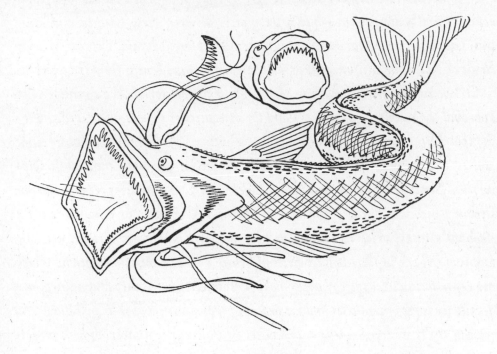

WE CAN RATIONALISE
these stories if we want to. When we read about the furry thighs of the Old Man
of the Sea we can nod to ourselves wisely and realise that we are dealing with a
touched-up story about one of the great apes of the East Indies, of Borneo or Sumatra, while on the other hand the apes who took possession of Sindbad's ship
of his Third Voyage seem much more likely to be members of a Negrito tribe,
with their yellow eyes and their black faces: Andamanese, most likely. We
can note that Sindbad's adventure with the cannibal giant has an almost exact par-
allel in the Odyssey, and that even in Irish and Scandinavian folklore there are
stories about whales being mistaken for islands. The funeral rites described in
the Fourth Voyage may be a scrambled mixture of descriptions of two different
customs; you can catch echoes of the Indian suttee and possibly also (I fancy) of

somebody's account of his premature burial in a Parsee Tower of Silence. We can even, if we want to, explain away the Roc by suggesting that some early explorer actually penetrated far enough into the waters between New Guinea and Australia as to see, or to hear stories about, the moa before it became extinct. We can do all of these things if we want to, and some of us may benefit from the exercise.

Or we can be more literary in our estimate of the stories. We can note with approval the simplicity of the style and the directness of the narrative, remembering that Defoe made use of the same devices with equal effect. We can observe the artless touches of local color which convey realism, as when the newly ship-wrecked Sindbad took note that both Chinese and Comarin aloes grew beside the stream which was to carry him to new adventures, or when he remarks that the elephant's tusks which he carried to Haroun Al-Rachid were fifteen feet long and two feet six in their longest circumference. Those of the conversations which are reported in direct speech have somehow retained their vitality and naturalness despite the lapse of centuries and the ordeal of translation and re-translation, and we can try if we like to see how this effect is achieved, remembering how consci-entiously recent writers have worked to attain the same ends and to overthrow the pompous tradition of the Victorians. There are the brief bits of incidental descrip-tion—fish with the heads of owls and the bird born from a sea shell (a distant relative of the barnacle goose)—which keep the reader interested (as Herodotus also discovered) as well as maintaining him in a mood of readiness to accept the fantastic. We can be aware of all these things and yet we can be quite certain that the writer never once, consciously or self-consciously, made deliberate use of such tricks, although Robert Louis Stevenson did.

Sindbad is very much a human being, and a typical man of his time. His thoughts are tinged by the fatalism and resignation of Mohammedanism, and yet he displays the restlessness and energy which carried that religion from one end of the Old World to the other in two centuries. He is charitable, even generous, and yet desperately self-centered. He can actually note that his shipmates are honest and good-hearted—"*of the kind who can live contentedly together and render aid when aid is needed*"—*yet he never utters a word of regret when these selfsame companions are roasted on spits, and drowned, and swallowed by snakes. He kills the new arrivals in the living tomb so that he can eat their provisions without sharing them, and when he finds a way of escape it does not occur to him to leave behind any signpost to help those unfortunates who will come later. He accepts, almost without comment, the extraordinary charity and honesty of the various sea captains with whom he comes in contact (although in this connection we must make allowance for the strongly felt brotherhood of Islam), but he is not beyond a little sharp practice himself. He is both resolute and smug, restless and resigned, and we cannot help but like him.*

Traditionally, these tales were told by the professional story-teller amid the heat and din and dust and stink of the street, hammered out by question and answer as such stories always are:

"*Once upon a time there was a man—*"
"*What sort of man?*"
"*A young man—*"
"*Who was his father?*"
"*A poor potter—*"
"*Where did he live?*"

—and so on, interminably, with intervals when the narrator has reached an interesting point and passes 'round his wooden bowl for payment before continuing. Yet this is hard to believe; the stories are not merely too good, but they have the wrong flavor. The ogre-story is too closely related to the Greek, and the local color is too correct and apropos; and, if we care (there is not the least reason why we should) to probe into the history of the manuscript sources through which these stories reached Europe, our doubts are intensified. I have the feeling that these particular stories are mainly the work of one man. He may have sought inspiration in the market-place,

he may have read Greek (or, far more likely, listened to tales told by a prisoner captured from the tottering Greek Empire) and he may—possibly as a child—have listened to stories told by gray-bearded magnates of the Califate, but he made his stories his own as Shakespeare did, or as O. Henry did, or as Damon Runyon did. He impressed his own art and personality upon them, and he must have been a man of supreme genius. Most of the books written about Shakespeare for instance demonstrate the futility of trying to make deductions from the allusions in his work regarding the course of the life of the writer of those works when they are fiction, and I would not dream of trying to pry further; I like to think of my unknown author—Arab or Persian or Syrian—writing his stories out of sheer creative joy and with a perfect disregard for the contemporary Mohammedan religious contempt for stories told merely for entertainment.

It was a time when the world was expanding, a period of renaissance resulting from a new mingling of cultures around the eastern end of the Mediterranean to which Persian and Greek and Syrian and Arab all contributed in consequence of the Mohammedan conquests. During the centuries immediately preceding, the tenuous link with the Far East which had been maintained by the Romans had disappeared; under the Califate a far more substantial connection was built up. A new world lay open to the Mohammedan adventurers and they poured into it, carrying their culture and their religion all the way to the Pacific. Missionary zeal—as is evident from Sindbad—was subordinate to the desire for profit, but the profits offered incentive enough. There is always far more money to be made out of the luxuries than out of the necessities of life, and it is the luxuries provided by any new country which are first dealt in, as is well illustrated by the history of the fur trade in the North American continent. Pepper and cinnamon, jewels and sandalwood and camphor, these were what the adventurers sought and found. From their main emporium in Baghdad they had first to negotiate the tricky river navigation to Basra; and beyond that lay five hundred miles of the Persian Gulf with its sandbanks and its rocks and its sudden gales, its pearl fisheries and its intolerable climate. More-

over, no sooner had a profitable trade developed in the Gulf than pirates began to prey upon it, based mainly on the Arabian side: Mohammedans with small scruples about robbing their brethren of the Faith. But at the Strait of Ormuz the merchant adventurers left these terrors behind them and entered upon the wide Indian Ocean where the regularity of the monsoons made possible extensive voyages with only the crudest of navigational aids. They explored the African coast as far south as Zanzibar; they knew the Indian coast from Scinde to Ceylon, whose pearls competed with those of Bahrein. At various entrepôts of trade in this direction they exchanged their goods for those of the Far East. But the hardier spirits among them, disdaining to pay a middle-man his profits, pushed into the Bay of Bengal and beyond, to find themselves among the enchanted waters of the East Indies. They had some sort of acquaintance with Sumatra and Java; they reached Timor, the Moluccas and the Philippines. It is possible that some of the camphor they brought back with them (camphor, like the ambergris of the Indian Ocean whales, was in constant demand as a basis for perfumes) they obtained at its main source, the island of Formosa.

The navigation of East Indian waters has its dangers even for vessels with modern equipment; those early adventurers suffered casualties in plenty—as witness Sindbad's numerous shipwrecks—which served to multiply the profits of the ultimate survivors. Captains found their way from place to place largely by rule of thumb, and the captain who had discovered a route to points where he could make profitable exchanges was in possession of a valuable trade secret which he was not likely to impart to anyone else. Nor was he, presumably, above misleading his competitors, and accounting for his movements and the spoils he brought home with him by tales hardly more fantastic than the reality appeared to him. Maybe it was someone with a vivid imagination, and who had developed a profitable business in Indian diamonds, who started the story about the Roc being used to recover diamonds from an inaccessible valley: for the story is clearly grafted on to earlier legends. In any case the trade secrets would be whispered about and exaggerated by rumor, even when the travelers did not try to impress the stay-at-homes by coloring their accounts of their experiences. So we get accounts of the sources of camphor and ambergris which are not far from the truth, side by side with fantastic yarns of fish that swallow ships.

Perhaps it is a pity that men who dealt so constantly with the marvelous should not have considered it necessary to describe the matter-of-fact. Sindbad passes over the technical details lightly. What kind of ships did he sail in? How were they rigged and how were they manned and what equipment did they carry? We would be glad to know what provisions were carried on these prodigious voyages. Was the drinking water carried in skins or in barrels? We know that, as always at sea, fresh water was precious, but that is only by deduction from the fact that one of the first things the ship's company did when they landed on the whale island was to wash their clothes—Sindbad owed his life to the wooden wash-trough somebody took ashore for that express purpose—but we do not know what the water ration was nor how it was doled out. Sindbad knew nothing about the primitive art of navigation as practiced in those days, and probably all that was known was kept a guarded secret. It would be interesting to know what the captain was really doing on the last voyage when, a week out from Karachi, they approached the Clime of Kings and he tried to ascertain where they were. He climbed the mast; captains have done that since before history began. But then he took something "like ashes" from his sea chest and wetted it and sniffed it, and then he referred to a little book. The little book we can explain; presumably it was navigational instructions compiled on previous voyages either by himself or his predecessors. But what was it that he sniffed at? My own theory is that they had been taking casts with an armed lead, and that what Sindbad is really describing is the examination of the sample of the sea bottom brought up by the tallow at the bottom of the lead. Where they were at this moment, and what were the dangerous waters which moved the captain to such despair, can only be the subject of even wilder surmise. The next place that Sindbad positively identifies is Ceylon; but, as he arrived there on a river that flowed under a mountain, we have to seek some intermediate point and we can find it in the Laccadive Islands, to this day a serious menace to navigation off the west coast of India.

And here we are rationalising Sindbad's adventures all over again, which is a waste of time and effort. It is the stories themselves which should claim our whole attention—the constant flow of incident, the charm of the narrative, and the artless pictures which they draw of a younger world.

C. S. FORESTER

CONTENTS

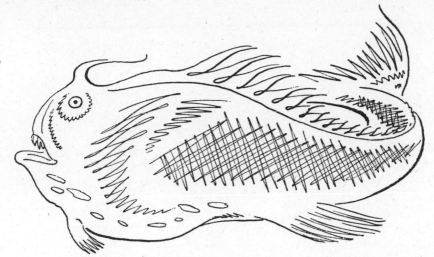

THE

SEVEN VOYAGES

OF

SINDBAD THE SAILOR

PROLOGUE

IT IS RELATED,
that there lived in Baghdad, during the reign of the khalifat Haroun Al-Rachid, a poor man called Sindbad the Porter, who earned
his living by carrying loads upon his head. One day, as he was
sweating and staggering in the great heat under a more than usually
heavy burden, he passed the door of a house which seemed to him
to belong to some rich merchant, as the ground about it was well
swept and refreshed with rose-water. The breeze blew soft and cool
there and a bench stood near the door for tired wayfarers, so Sindbad set his load upon the ground and sat down on the bench to
breathe the scented air. He heard the concerted playing and singing
of lutes and voices skilled in the craft of song, and the mingled jar-
gonning of doves, nightingales, blackbirds, bulbuls, pigeons, and
tame partridges, praising Allah in sweet modes. He marvelled in
his soul and, for very pleasure, passed his head through the opening of the door and saw a great garden, filled with a press of slaves,
servants, and guests, and furnished as only are furnished the gardens of kings.

The smell of admirable meats came to him, mingled with wafts
of open wine; so that he could not help sighing and crying: "Glory

be to the Creator and Giver of all things, who parts His gifts as it pleases Him! O my God, if I cry to You it is not to call Your justice and Your generosity in question, for the creature may not criticise the Master! but simply to witness what I have seen. Glory be to Him who makes men high and lowly, for He has a reason, though we may not see it. The master of this house is very happy, living in a delight of odours, and meats and more than exquisite wines. He is joyous and calm, and there are others like him; while I am hot and tired and poor and miserable!"

Stirred to his depths by such thoughts, the porter made up these stanzas and sang them at the top of his voice:

> *I have heard of poor men waking*
> *In the shadow of a palace,*
> *But the solace of such waking*
> *Is not for me.*
>
> *I have seen the rich man's burden,*
> *Heavy gold on gold increasing;*
> *But the blessing of that burden*
> *Is not for me.*
>
> *Though more heavy than those others,*
> *Is the load which makes me weary,*
> *What I carry is for others,*
> *Is not for me.*
>
> *Yet when I have heard complaining*
> *Of the equity of Allah,*
> *I thank Allah such complaining*
> *Is not for me!*

When Sindbad the porter had finished singing, he rose and was about to take up his burden again when the door of the palace opened and a kind-faced little slave, having an exquisite body sumptuously dressed, came up to him and took him by the hand, saying: "My master wishes to see you: follow me." The porter was afraid at this invitation and vainly tried to find some excuse for not going. At length he was constrained to leave his load with the door-keeper and follow the child into the interior of the building.

He saw a wonderful house filled with grave and noble people and, when he was led into the great central hall, came upon an honourable company of well-born guests. There were flowers of all kinds, perfumes of every sweetness, great selection of dry conserves, sweetmeats, almond paste, and rare fruits; there were innumerable dishes loaded with roast lambs and other delicate meat, and jars past counting full of wine from a chosen grape. There were fair slaves ranged in due order bending over lutes and, in the middle among the guests, sat a tall and dignified old man, with a white beard, a kind and handsome face, and an expression of calm nobility.

The porter stood stock-still in his amazement, saying to himself: "As Allah lives, this must be the palace of some Jinni or some very mighty king!" He hastened to adopt the attitude demanded by polite breeding and, after wishing peace to all and calling down blessings upon them, stood modestly with lowered head.

The old man begged him to approach and sit down by his side; after a courteous speech of welcome, he had food and drink brought and not until his new guest had eaten, thanked Allah, and washed his hands, did he allow himself to put a question to him:

"Be very welcome; be at your ease; be happy upon this day! Will you allow me to ask your name and your trade?" "O master," replied the other, "I am called Sindbad the Porter, and I carry heavy loads for light payment." The master of the house smiled, saying: "O porter, your name is the same as mine; for I am called Sindbad the Sailor. . . . I requested you to come to me because I wished you to sing again those delightful stanzas which I heard you utter when you were sitting outside my door."

The porter was confused at this and hastened to say: "In the name of Allah, do not blame me too much for my inconsiderate singing, for grief, weariness, and misery may give birth to rudeness, foolishness, and insolence in the best of us." "Do not be at all ashamed to have sung in such a manner," said Sindbad the Sailor to Sindbad the Porter, "be perfectly at ease here for you are my brother. I pray you to sing your verses again, for they surprised me by their beauty."

The porter sang the song which you have already heard, and Sindbad the Sailor turned in delight to the singer, saying: "My destiny also makes a strange tale, which I will tell you. When you have heard all my adventures, you will understand what trials and vicissitudes I have had to undergo to reach the felicity of this palace; you will realise that I have had to purchase the wealth which sustains my age with strange and terrible labours, with calamities, misfortunes, and hardships which are scarcely credible. I have accomplished seven extraordinary voyages and the narrative of each one is enough to stupefy the listeners with an excess of marvel. And yet all that I tell you had been written for me by Destiny: for all things so written must inevitably come to pass."

THE FIRST VOYAGE

YOU MUST KNOW, MY noble guests, and you, O honourable porter who bear the same name as myself, that my father was a great merchant who wisely gave to the poor and, on his death, left me a considerable fortune in money, land, and villages.

These things came into my disposition when I reached manhood and straightway I set myself to eat strange meats and drink unusual wines, to frequent the youth of my own age, to wear each day a fortune upon my back in clothes, and to cultivate the art of friendship. For a long time I lived in this way thinking that nothing could abate my patrimony; until one morning I suddenly recovered my senses on finding that I had practically nothing left. I grew afraid lest I should have to pass my old age in poverty and called to mind certain words of our master, Sulayman, son of David (on whom be prayer and peace!) which my dead father was fond of repeating: *The day of death is better than the day of birth, a living dog is better than a dead lion, and the grave is better than poverty.*

Therefore I rose up and, collecting the little which remained to me of furniture and garments, I sold it at auction together with the small holdings and few acres which I had not spent; and thus gained the sum of three thousand dirhams. With this sum I determined to travel, for I remembered the words of the poet:

> *What is success?*
> *The deathless daughter*
> *Of your weariness.*
> *It is to dive in deeper, deeper water,*

And ever deeper, layer on layer
Of cold green mystery,
For an ever rosier, ever whiter, ever greyer
Pearl of the sea.

I ran to the market and bought myself a lading of varied merchandise which I had carried on board a ship just starting from Baghdad with other merchants. Being determined to put to sea, I rejoiced to feel the boat dropping down stream from Baghdad to the port of Bassora.

From Bassora we sailed, day after day, night after night, over the sea, visiting island after island and land after land, selling or bartering our goods at each.

One day, after some weeks of sailing out of sight of land, we saw an island in the sea with such fair greenery that it appeared like one of the gardens of Eden. At once the captain made towards this delectable land and, when the anchor had been cast and the ladder lowered, allowed his passengers to disembark.

All of us merchants landed, carrying food and cooking utensils with us. Some lit fires and prepared a meal, others washed their linen, and others again contented themselves with resting or walking. I was among the last and, without neglecting either food or drink, found time to wander among the trees and take pleasure in the strange vegetation.

We were all occupied in these various ways, when the island suddenly shook throughout its length so violently that we were thrown to the ground. While we lay dazed, we saw the captain appear in the bows of his ship and heard him cry in an agonised voice with wild gesturings: "Save yourselves! Come aboard for your lives!

THE "ISLAND" SUBMERGES

That is no island but a gigantic whale! She has lived in the middle of this sea since time was young and the trees have grown in the sea sand upon her back. You have troubled her repose by lighting fires upon her; now she is moving! Come aboard for your lives, before she sinks in the water and destroys you all!"

Hearing these cries of the captain, the merchants left all they had; clothes, cooking pots, and ovens; and rushed towards the ship which was already weighing anchor. Some of them reached her in time, others did not; for the whale, after bounding terrifically two or three times, sank like lead in the water and involved those who were still upon her back beneath monstrous waves.

I was one of these last, but Allah saved me from drowning by guiding a piece of hollow wood towards me, a kind of large trough in which some of the passengers had been washing their linen. First I clung to it and then managed to get astride it by more than human efforts which danger and the dear love of life made possible for me. When I was well fixed, I began to beat the water with my feet as if they had been sculls and made some progress, though my frail craft was canted to right and left by the force of the waves.

By this time the captain was making off with all sails set, leaving those who had not been able to reach the vessel to perish. I rowed as hard as I could with my feet after the disappearing ship until, when at last she dropped below the horizon and night fell, I gave myself up for lost. All that night and the next I fought against the sea and at last wind and wave brought me to the coast of a steep island covered with climbing plants which fell sheer down the face of the cliffs and trailed in the water. With immense labour of feet and hands I managed to climb up the branches and ropes of these plants until I reached the top of the cliff.

Being now certain of my safety, I examined the state of my body and found that not only was it covered with wounds and bruises, but that my feet were swelled and marred by bites of fishes who had filled their bellies with all of me which they could reach. Previous to this examination I had felt no pain, being rendered numb with

fatigue and danger, but now I threw myself down on the earth of the island and was soon plunged in a deep swoon.

I remained thus without motion or consciousness until, on the second day, I was awakened by the sun beating down upon my face. I tried to rise, but my feet would not bear me and I fell back upon the ground. I felt in woeful case, but managed to drag myself, sometimes upon my feet and hands, sometimes walking with my knees, until I came at last to a plain covered with fruit trees and watered by pure streams.

There I rested for many days, eating and drinking, until my soul grew stronger and the pains of my body easier. At last I was able to move about with the help of a pair of wooden crutches which I made for myself; and I would spend my time hobbling among the trees, musing, eating fruit, and admiring the handiwork of All-Powerful Allah.

One day, as I went along the shore, I saw far off something which I took at first for a savage beast or some monster of the sea. Its appearance so interested me that although I was in two minds whether it was safe to do so, I went forward towards it. At last I could see that the animal was a mare of marvellous breed fastened to a stake upon the shore. She was so excellent a mount that I was on the point of going up quite close to her, when a sudden cry halted me where I was and a man sprang, as it were, from the earth and ran towards me crying: "Who are you? Where do you come from? What led you to venture into this place?"

"Good master," I answered, "I am a stranger who was voyaging on a ship and was cast into the sea with certain other passengers. Allah saved me by means of a wooden trough and I was thrown by the waves upon your shore."

The man took my hand, saying: "Follow me." So I followed him, and he led me down into a cave below the earth which contained a great hall where he caused me to sit in a place of honour and gave me food. I ate till I was satisfied; when my spirits were a little calmer, the man asked me for my story and I told it from beginning to end, to his great and unfeigned astonishment. "In the name of Allah, my master," I added, "do not blame me if I, who

31

have told you the whole truth, now ask you why you dwell in this underground cave and why that mare is fastened all alone on the sea shore."

The man answered: "There are many of us in this island, posted in different spots to look after the horses of King Mihrajan. Every month, at the new moon, we each take a virgin blood-mare down to the shore and, after fastening her securely, hide in our caves. We have not long to wait, before a sea-horse, attracted by the odour of the female, comes up out of the water and, after looking to left and right to see that no one is by, goes up to the mare and covers her. When he has finished he gets off her back and tries to lead her away with him; when she cannot follow him, he whinnies loudly and strikes her with his head and hoofs; this noise is a signal for us that he has finished covering her, so we rush out and converge towards him, uttering loud cries which drive him back into the sea. The mare becomes pregnant, and, in course of time, drops a foal worth all of a king's treasure. The sea-horse is due today; as soon as his work is over, I will present you to King Mihrajan and show you our country. Blessed be Allah who caused us to meet, for without me you would have perished of grief in this desert place and never have seen your native land again!"

I heartily thanked the groom and was still talking to him when suddenly the sea-horse came out of the water, threw himself upon the mare, and covered her. When he had finished, he would have taken her away with him, but she could only rear, neighing all round the circle of her picket. My friend leapt from the cave, and calling his companions, led them towards the sea-horse with loud cries and a clashing of swords against shields, so that the frightened beast plunged like a buffalo into the sea and disappeared.

The other grooms crowded round me and greeted me amiably, offering me food and drink and a good horse to ride on. I accepted their invitation and we all set off together towards the king's palace. When we reached the city, my companions went first into the royal presence to announce my arrival and later, when an interview had been granted to me, I was led before King Mihrajan and wished him peace.

He returned my greeting, welcomed me kindly, and asked to hear my story from my own lips. I told him every detail of my adventures so that he marvelled, saying: "My son, as Allah lives you would certainly not have survived such terrible trials if a long life had not been written for you. Praise be to Allah for your deliverance!" He reassured me with further benevolent words, admitted me into the number of his friends, and, as proof of his regard, appointed me inspector of ports and bays and registrar of shipping.

My new duties were not so arduous as to prevent me seeing the king every day; he soon came to prefer me above all his friends and to load me with daily gifts; and I had so much influence over him that eventually every affair of the kingdom passed through my hands, to the general good of the people.

But, amid all these honours and duties, I did not forget my own country or quite lose hope of some day returning to it. I used to ask each passenger and sailor if he knew in what direction lay the city of Baghdad; but none could answer me or say with truth that they had heard of the place. Therefore the longer I stayed in this foreign land, the sadder I became for my home and the greater grew my surprise that no sea captain could show me a way of return.

While I lived in that isle, I had occasion to hear and see many astonishing things; I will tell you a few of them:

One day, while I was in the presence of King Mihrajan, I was introduced to certain Indians, who willingly answered the questions which I put to them, and informed me that, in their country, which is called India, there are a great number of castes, of which the two most important are Kshatriya and Brahman. The first is composed of well-born and equitable men, who are never guilty of sin or oppression; and the second of pure and holy people who never drink wine and yet are friends of joy, of good manners, of horses, of pageantry, and beauty. The learned Indians also told me that these castes are divided into seventy-two lesser castes, whose traditions are separate in every way. This astonished me a great deal. Also I had occasion to visit a neighbouring land belonging to my king, which was called Kabil. This place resounds with the beating of drums and cymbals on every night of the year and yet I found that the inhabitants were of logical mind and given to beautiful thoughts. In those far seas I once saw a fish more than a hundred cubits long and observed other lesser fish with the heads of owls. Many and strange were the prodigies which I saw there but it would be wearisome to multiply them in my story. Suffice it to say that I lived long enough in that island to learn many things and to become very rich by judicious bargaining.

One day, as I was standing by the shore, leaning upon my stick and watching for vessels as my duty was, I saw a great ship enter the bay. I waited till she had cast anchor and lowered her ladder and then, going aboard, interviewed the captain to take an inventory of his cargo. The sailors unloaded her in my presence, while I listed the various merchandise and, when their work was over, I asked the captain if he had anything more aboard. "My master," he answered, "I have still a quantity of merchandise in the hold, but it is in storage, as the owner who came with us was drowned during the voyage. When opportunity serves, I shall sell his property and take the money back to his relations in Baghdad, the City of Peace."

"O captain, what was the name of that merchant?" I cried with a fast-beating heart. "Sindbad the Sailor," he answered. I looked more closely at the man and saw that he was indeed the captain who had had to abandon us upon the whale. "I am Sindbad the Sailor!" I cried at the top of my voice; and then continued: "When the whale moved under the fires that were lighted on her back I was thrown into the water, but, thanks to a wooden trough which some of the merchants had used for washing their clothes, was able to ride upon the sea and paddle with my feet. After that there happened that which Allah permitted to happen." Straightway I told the captain how I had been saved and through the course of what trials I had risen to the post of marine registrar under King Mihrajan.

When the captain heard my words, he cried: "There is no power or might save in Allah! In none of his creatures have I ever found honesty or an upright heart. How do you dare, O wily registrar, to pretend to be Sindbad the Sailor, when we all saw him drowned with our own eyes? Are you not ashamed of such an impudent lie?"

"Indeed, good captain," I answered, "lies are the weapon of the deceitful. Listen, for I will give you proofs that I am indeed that drowned Sindbad of whom you speak." Then I reminded him of certain details, known only to myself and him, of that calamity which I have already described to you. At last he could doubt no longer, so he called together the other merchants, and they all congratulated me on my safety, saying: "As Allah lives, we could hardly believe at first that you had not been drowned. Surely He has given you a second life!"

The captain delivered all my merchandise to me and, after examining it to see that nothing was missing and that my name and seal on each bale had not been interfered with, I had it carried to the market and sold the greater part of it at a profit of a hundred for one, reserving only certain rich pieces as a present for King Mihrajan. When the king heard of the ship's arrival he raised his hands in astonishment and, as he loved me much, refused to be outdone in generosity by me, making me presents of great price. I hastened to sell these for a considerable fortune in money which I caused to be carried on board the very ship in which I had first set out.

When all my preparations were made, I thanked the king for his protection and great generosity. He gave me leave to depart in many sad and touching words and made me further costly presents, which I did not sell and which you can see about you in this hall, O honourable guests. As a final cargo I sent aboard a great supply of those perfumes which you can smell even at this moment, aloe-wood, camphor, incense, and sandal, in which that far isle abounded.

We set sail and Allah sent us favourable breezes so that after many nights and days we arrived in sight of Bassora and, without delaying long at that port, continued up stream and joyfully cast anchor at Baghdad, the City of Peace, the place of my birth.

I soon came, loaded with riches and ready with great presents, to my own house in my own street, and found the folk of my family in excellent health. I hastened to buy many slaves of both sexes, mamelukes, beautiful veiled women, negroes, lands, houses, and other property, more in number than I had inherited on the death of my father.

In this new life I forgot the sorrows, hardships, and dangers which I had undergone, the sadness of exile and the fatigues of voyaging.

I made charming friends and lived a life of calm joy for many months, feasting my mind with pleasure, eating delicately, and drinking rare wines.

Such was the first of my voyages.

Tomorrow, if Allah wills, I will give you all an account of the second of my seven voyages; I can assure you that it is much more extraordinary than the first.

Sindbad the Sailor asked Sindbad the Porter to dine with him and at last sent him away with a hundred pieces of gold, begging him to return on the morrow, saying: "I shall look forward with delight to further acquaintance with your urbanity and charming manners." "Be it upon my head and before my eye!" answered the porter, "I beg respectfully to accept. I pray that joy may be everlasting in your house, my master!"

With that he returned home, marvelling and rejoicing; and dreamed all night of what he had heard and experienced in the house of Sindbad the Sailor.

In the morning the porter returned to the house of Sindbad the Sailor, who received him affably, saying: "May you find friendship easy in this house and be altogether at home with me." The porter wished to kiss his host's hand and, when Sindbad the Sailor would not permit this, cried: "May Allah whiten your days and establish His blessing about you for ever!" When the other guests arrived all sat down about a loaded cloth, rich with roast lambs and golden with fowls which lay among bowls of delicious stuffing and pistachio paste and were flanked by abundance of nuts and grapes. They ate and drank and bathed their spirits in the melody of skilful lute-players. When the feasting was over the guests fell silent and Sindbad spoke to them of:

THE SECOND VOYAGE

I WAS LIVING A LIFE
of unexpected pleasure when, one day, the old desire entered my
head to visit far countries and strange people; to voyage among the
isles and curiously regard things hitherto unknown to me; also the
trading habit rose in me again. I went to the market and spent a
great deal of money on suitable merchandise which I had solidly
packed and taken to the quay, where I soon found a fair new ship,
equipped with excellent sails, having every sort of marine mecha-
nism aboard and a stout crew of excellent sailors. I fell in love with
this vessel and caused all my goods to be taken aboard and placed
with those of other merchants who were known to me and with
whom I was very pleased to journey.

We set sail the same day and made excellent time across the sea,
visiting from island to island and ocean to ocean for many weeks,
making ourselves known to the notables and chief merchants at
each port of call and both selling and exchanging our goods to great
advantage. Fate willed that we should touch at an island of great

natural beauty, covered with tall trees, rich in fruits and flowers, filled with the singing of birds, watered by cool streams, but utterly uninhabited.

The captain willingly fell in with our wish to spend a few hours in this place, so we cast anchor and, going on shore, began to walk up and down, breathing the good air of the shady and bird-haunted meadows. Taking a little food with me, I went and sat down by the side of a clear stream, shadowed from the sun by thick leafage, and took great pleasure in eating and drinking in such surroundings. A small breeze whispered an invitation to perfect rest, so I lay upon the grass and let sleep and the cool and scented air overcome my eyelids.

When I woke I saw none of my fellow-travellers and soon discovered that the ship had left without anyone noticing my absence. I looked to right and left, before and behind, and could see no moving thing save the white sail dipping far out to sea.

So great was my grief and stupefaction that I felt my bile duct on the point of bursting. What would become of me on this desert island, seeing that all I possessed was being swiftly carried away from me by the ship? A prey to desolate thoughts, I cried aloud: "All is lost, O Sindbad the Sailor! If a kind destiny saved you on your first voyage, you cannot expect her to do the same again. The cup which falls a second time is sure to break."

I wept and groaned, I uttered great cries to break the despair which seemed to be closing round my heart. I beat my head with my hand, crying: "O miserable fool, why did you so rashly tempt the sea again, when you were living in all delight at Baghdad? Was not your meat, your drink, your clothing all that could be desired? Was there any happiness which you lacked? Was it as if your first

39

voyage had been unsuccessful? . . . We belong to Allah and all return to Him at last." With that, I threw myself upon the earth and all but went mad.

At length, realising that my regrets were useless and my repentance a thought too late, I rose to my feet and, after wandering aimlessly for some time, climbed to the top of a tree to avoid any deadly meeting with wild beasts or unknown enemy. From that perch I looked long to left and right, but could see nothing save the sky, the earth, the sea, the birds, the sands, and the rocks. Happening, however, to look in a different direction, I noticed on the far horizon the appearance of something white and enormous. I climbed down from my tree; but, being a little frightened, it was only slowly and very carefully that I made my way towards the strange thing which I had noticed. At length I drew near enough to see that it was a gigantic dome of shining white, with a broad base and yet taller than it was broad. I walked all round it but could find no door of any sort; then I tried to climb up the side of it, but it was so polished and slippery that I could make no progress. At last I had to content myself with measuring the thing and, taking a mark by my footsteps in the sand, walked round it again and found that it had a diameter of exactly a hundred and fifty paces.

While I was racking my brains to think of some way by which I could enter this dome, I suddenly saw the sun disappear and the day about me change to night. At first I thought a great cloud had passed before the sun, although such a thing would have been impossible in midsummer; therefore I lifted my head to examine so unseasonable a portent and observed an enormous bird, with formidable wings, flying in the eye of the sun.

I could not believe my eyes until I recalled that travellers and sailors had told me in my youth that there existed, in a far island, a bird of terrifying size called the Roc; a bird which could lift an elephant. I concluded then that this must be a Roc and that the white dome, at whose foot I found myself, was none other than one of its eggs. I was soon proved right in my supposition, for the bird came to earth over the egg, covering it completely, stretching its great wings on either side and letting its two feet touch the earth to left and right. In this attitude it went to sleep. (Blessed be He who sleeps not throughout eternity!)

I had been lying flat on my belly upon the earth and now found myself below one of the bird's feet which, seen thus close, seemed larger than the trunk of an old tree. Rising swiftly, I undid the stuff of my turban and, after having doubled it and twisted it into a strong rope, tied it in a firm knot about my waist and about one of the toes of the Roc. For I thought to myself: "This monstrous bird will sometime fly away and, when he does so, I will be carried into some place where I can see others of my kind again. Wherever I am set down will be better than a desert island."

In spite of my movements, the bird took no more notice of me than if I had been a trivial fly or modest crawling ant.

I remained as I was all night, not daring to close my eyes lest the bird should fly away with me while I was asleep; but it was not till morning that it stepped from the egg, uttered a terrible cry, and soared into the air. It rose and rose until I thought that I was about to touch the vault of Heaven, then suddenly dropped so swiftly that I could not feel my own weight, and came to earth with me. It lighted upon a jut of rock and at once, with trembling fingers, I untied my turban, fearing that the bird might rise with me again before I could free myself. As soon as I was clear of the claw, I shook

myself and arranged my garments; I was hurrying to place myself
out of reach of my unconscious liberator, when it took the air
again, this time carrying in its talons a vast black thing, a very great
serpent of detestable appearance. Soon it disappeared in the direction of the sea.

I looked round this new region to which I had come and was fixed
to the spot on which I stood with fear, for I found myself in a wide
and deep valley shut in on all sides by mountains so high that, when
I looked at their tops, my turban fell off behind. They were so pre-
cipitous that to climb them would have been impossible and I saw
that nothing was to be gained by making the attempt.

My despair was complete and I cried: "Oh, how much better it
would have been to stay in that deserted island than to come to this
barren place where there is neither food nor water; there at least I
had the advantage of fruit trees and delightful streams, but here are
nothing but unfriendly rocks among which I shall die of hunger and
thirst. There is no power or might save in Allah! I escape from one
evil, to fall into a greater and more certain!"

I walked about to take stock of the valley and found that its rocks
were all of diamond. The earth about me was littered with diamonds, great and small, which had fallen from the mountains and,
in some places, made heaps as high as a man's head.

I was just beginning to take an interest in these stones when I
saw a sight more fearful than all the horrors I had already experienced. The guardians of the diamond rocks were moving about
their treasure; innumerable black snakes, thicker and longer than
palm-trees, each one of which could have swallowed a large elephant.
They were beginning to go back into their dens, for by day they hid
themselves from their enemy the Roc and only moved about at night.

SINDBAD AND THE ROC

With infinite precautions I began to move away from the place where they seemed thickest, examining every inch of ground before I set my foot on it, and saying to myself: "This is what you get for abusing the patience of Destiny, O Sindbad, O man with empty and insatiable eyes!" In a state of pitiable fear I continued to move up and down the valley, resting from time to time in the most sheltered places I could find, until the fall of night.

I had forgotten all about food and drink and had no other thought than to save my life from the serpents; at last I found a narrow-mouthed cave near the place where I had been set down by the Roc. I crawled through the entrance and then rolled a stone against it on the inside. I crawled forward, with my fear somewhat abated, looking for a comfortable place to sleep, and thinking: "Tomorrow at dawn I will go out and see what Destiny has in store for me."

I was about to lie down when I noticed what I had taken for a large black rock in the middle of the cave was a terrible snake, rolled about her eggs; my skin shrivelled like a dead leaf with fear and I fell senseless to the ground, where I remained until morning.

Coming to myself and finding that I had not been devoured in the night, I found strength to roll away the stone and totter like a drunken man into the open air; I was so worn out with lack of sleep and food that my legs could hardly bear me up. I was looking about me when suddenly I saw a great joint of meat flatten itself with a noisy slap upon the rocks beside me; I started and lifted my eyes to see who bombarded me in this fashion, but could perceive no one. Then a memory flashed across my mind of something I had heard from merchant-adventurers and explorers who had visited the diamond mountains. It seemed that men, who wished to take diamonds from this inaccessible valley, had the curious practice of cutting

sheep into quarters and throwing them from the top of the mountain, so that the diamonds on which they fell pierced them and became fixed in them. Soon Rocs and mighty eagles would swoop
upon this provision and carry it from the valley in their claws to
their nests in the high hills. Then the jewellers would throw themselves upon the birds, with great cries and beating of their arms, so
that they were obliged to let fall their prize and fly away. After that
the men had only to explore the quarters of meat and pick out the
diamonds.

46

With this memory, a plan came to me which might just succeed in saving me from the living tomb of the valley. First I selected a great quantity of diamonds, choosing always the largest and most valuable, and hid them about me everywhere. I filled my pockets with them, let them fall down between my robe and my shirt, stuffed my turban and my drawers with them, and pressed them into the lining of my garments.

After that I unrolled the stuff of my turban as I had done before and, lying down below the quarter of mutton, bound it solidly to my chest. I had not lain long in this position when I felt myself lifted like a feather by the formidable talons of a Roc which were fastened in the meat. In the twinkling of an eye I was out of the valley and in the nest which my captor had built high in the mountains. Here the bird began to rip up the meat and my own flesh in order to feed her young with it. Happily for me a great clamour arose almost at once and the bird flew away, so that I was able to unfasten myself and stand upright with my face and clothes all bloody.

I saw a merchant hurrying to the spot whose face fell and became afraid as he saw me; however, when I did not move or make any hostile demonstration, he hurriedly bent over the meat and examined it, without finding any diamonds. Then he lifted his arms to the sky, crying: "O loss, O disillusion! There is no power save in Allah! I take refuge in Allah against the Evil One!" With that he clapped his hands together in an ecstasy of despair.

I wished him peace; but, instead of returning my greeting, he gave me a furious glance and said: "Who are you? And by what right have you come here to steal my goods?" "Do not be afraid, worthy merchant," I answered, "I am not a thief, and I have not touched your goods. Also I am a human being and not an evil Jinni as you appear to believe; I may even claim to be a very honest man, a merchant by profession, a man of strange adventures. As for my being here, it is a wonderful tale which I have to tell you. But first I wish to prove my benevolence towards you by asking you to accept some of these diamonds, which I myself picked up in that valley which no human has ever visited before."

I took some excellent stones from my belt, and gave them to the man, saying: "Here is such profit as you have never dared to hope for in all your life." Then the owner of the quarter of mutton was filled with joy and loaded me with a thousand effusive thanks, saying: "A blessing be upon you, O my master. A single one of these diamonds would be enough to make me rich until extreme old age, for never in my life have I seen the like even at the courts of kings." After further thanks he called to other merchants, who were among the near-by peaks, and they crowded round me, wishing me peace and welcome. I told them the whole of my strange adventures from beginning to end, but it would be useless to repeat it here.

When the good merchants had a little recovered from their surprise, they congratulated me upon my safety, saying: "As Allah lives, your destiny has drawn you alive out of an abyss from which no one before you has escaped." Then, seeing that I was dropping from hunger, thirst, and weariness, they gave me a plenitude of food and drink and, leading me to the tent which they occupied, watched over my sleep for a day and a night. On the second morning they led me down to the sea shore and I rejoiced as we went with exceeding joy over my two remarkable escapes. After a short voyage we came to a pleasant island covered with trees so great and shady that a hundred men could have escaped from the sun beneath one of them. From these trees is extracted that white substance of warm and agreeable odour which is called camphor. The tops of the trees are pierced and the sap, which is, as it were, the honey of the tree, falls, drop by drop, like gum, into vessels which are placed underneath to catch it.

In that island I also saw a terrible animal, which goes by the name

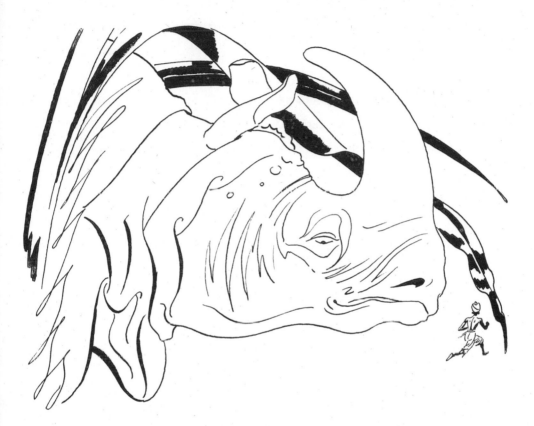

of *karkaddan* or rhinoceros. It pastures upon the meadows as a cow or buffalo; but is taller than a camel and carries a horn ten cubits long upon its snout. Upon this horn is engraved a human figure and it is so strong that with it the *karkaddan* fights and conquers the elephant, and at last spits and lifts it from the earth until it is dead.

49

But the fat of the elephant runs down into the eyes of the *karkaddan*, blinding it and causing it to fall down where it stands; then the terrible Roc swoops down upon both animals from the high air and carries them to its nest to feed its young. Also I saw many different kinds of buffaloes in that island.

We stayed there for some time, rejoicing in the excellent air, so that I had time to exchange some of my diamonds for a treasure of gold and silver too large to be contained in the hold of a single ship. At length we departed and, voyaging from island to island and from country to country and from city to city, at each of which we admired the beautiful works of God and made advantageous sales and exchanges, came at last to Bassora in the blessed land, and thence up the river to Baghdad, the home of peace. I hastened to my own house in my own street, loaded with riches, much golden money, and the finest of my diamonds; and, after being greeted rapturously by my friends and the folk of my family, distributed wealth to all, without forgetting the least of my acquaintances.

From that time forth I used life joyously, eating prime meats, drinking delicately, lying soft and dressing rich, and not denying myself the constant society of pleasant persons.

Every day important people came to hear me speak of my adventures and to learn how things went in far-off lands; and I rejoiced to entertain and teach them in the way they wished. They would never leave without first congratulating me on my escape from such terrible dangers and expressing gratifying surprise at all I told them. Such was my second voyage.

But tomorrow, my friends, if Allah wills, I will tell you the strange circumstances of my third periplus and you will find them far more interesting and breathless than those of my first two.

THE GUARDIANS OF THE DIAMONDS

Sindbad the Sailor fell silent and slaves hastened to set food and drink before his astonished guests. Finally Sindbad the Sailor gave a hundred gold pieces to Sindbad the Landsman, who took them with polite thanks and many blessings and came to his own house, his head turning with all the wonders which he had heard. In the morning the porter rose and, after making his prayer, returned, as he had been invited to do, to the house of the rich traveller. There he was welcomed cordially and bidden to take part in the daily feast and entertainment, which lasted till nightfall. Then, when the guests fell silent and attentive, Sindbad the Sailor told them of:

THE THIRD VOYAGE

YOU MUST KNOW, MY friends—but Allah has a greater knowledge than any of His creatures—that the comfortable life which I led after my return speedily made me forget all the dangers I had run and all the misfortunes which I had undergone, so that I began to grow tired of the monotonous laziness of my existence in Baghdad. My soul longed for change and the delights of travel and I was tempted anew by the love of skilful trading. Ambition is the cause of all misfortune, as I was soon to prove in a most terrible fashion. I bought a quantity of rich merchandise and took it from Baghdad to Bassora, where I found a great ship already filled with honest, good-hearted merchants, of the kind who can live contentedly together and render aid when aid is needed. I embarked with them in this vessel and we immediately set sail, with the blessing of Allah upon our voyage.

The happiest omens attended our setting forth and, in all the lands at which we touched, we both traded to advantage and learnt many new things, so that nothing was lacking to complete our happiness.

One day, when we were in mid-ocean far from any Mussulman country, we saw our captain, who had been closely examining the horizon, suddenly beat himself about the face, wrench out the hairs of his beard, tear his garments, and throw his turban to the deck.

We surrounded him, as he stood there weeping and lamenting, crying out: "What is it, captain?" "O passengers of peace," he answered, "the contrary wind has beaten us and thrown us from our course into a sinister sea. We are lost, for fate is driving us upon that island which you see before you and no man who ever touched there has returned alive to tell the tale. It is the Isle of Apes; and I feel deep in my soul that we are lost for ever."

As the captain was speaking, we saw our ship surrounded by a multitude of beings who were hairy like monkeys but more in number than an army of grasshoppers; while others, staying upon the beach, uttered howls which curdled our blood. We did not dare to attack these besiegers or try to repulse them, for fear they should rush upon us and kill us to a man, by the force of their number; for numbers in the end can overcome the most valorous. We made no movement while the apes climbed aboard and began to lay hands upon our belongings. They were more ugly than the most ugly of ugly things that I have seen in my life, being covered with hairs, having yellow eyes in black faces, and little bodies no more than three spans in height; their grimaces and cries were more terrible than the mind of man could have imagined. It was clear that they spoke to us and cursed us, grinding their jaws the while; but we could not understand their language, although we listened with our hearts in our mouths. As we stood helpless, they climbed up the masts, unfastened the sails, cutting the ropes with their teeth, and at last took possession of the helm. Guided by them and driven by the wind, our vessel soon beached herself and then the apes took us one by one and carried us to shore. Leaving us there, they climbed on board in a mass and, pushing off, were soon lost to sight in the open sea.

Our only means of transport being gone, we judged it useless to stand upon the sand, gazing upon the ocean, so we walked towards the middle of the island, where we found some fruit trees and a running stream, which would be sufficient to stave off an apparently certain death for many days.

While we were eating, we saw, far off among the trees, a great building which seemed to have been deserted by man.

We walked towards this building and found that it was a tall square palace, surrounded by solid walls in which a double door of ebony stood open. As no door-keeper stood there, we entered and found ourselves in a hall as large as most courtyards, furnished only with kitchen utensils of unusual size and great iron spits. The floor was heaped with mounds of bones, some of which were already white and others still fresh and juicy. A foul odour sickened our nostrils, but as we were worn out with weariness and fear, we threw ourselves down and slept.

The sun had hardly set when a noise like thunder woke us and we saw the figure of an enormous black man stepping down through the ceiling. He was taller than any palm-tree and uglier than all the apes put together. His eyes were red like two flaming ovens, his front teeth were long and curling like a boar's tusks, his mouth was as big as the mouth of a well, his lips lolled upon his breast, his ears fell over his shoulders like those of an elephant, and the ends of his fingers were taloned with lion's claws.

First we were convulsed with terror and then stayed very still, as the giant sat down on a bench beside the wall and examined us silently one by one. Finally he came up to us and, choosing me from among the others, seized me by the skin of my neck as if I had been a small parcel of cloth, and turned me this way and that, feeling me as a butcher feels a sheep's head. He apparently found me not to his liking, as I was sweaty with terror and yet little more than skin and bone because of the fatigues of my voyage. He threw me to the ground and treated my neighbour in the same way, only to put him aside and take up another. All of us were examined in this way and at last it came the captain's turn.

Now the captain was a fat and fleshy man, as well as being the tallest and strongest person aboard; therefore the giant preferred him to all others and, taking him between his fingers as a slaughter-man takes a lamb, broke his neck beneath his foot, spitted him on one of the great spits from mouth to anus, and lighting a great wood fire in the oven, turned him before it slowly until he was cooked to a nicety. After this the ogre pulled him to pieces with his finger-nails as if he had been a chicken and swallowed him in a few mouthfuls. Then he sucked and cracked the bones, throwing them to the floor as they were finished.

As soon as his meal was over, the giant stretched himself along the bench to digest it and was soon snoring like a buffalo. He slept thus till morning and then went away as he had come, leaving us half dead with fear.

When we were certain that he had really gone, we came out of the terrified silence, which we had maintained all night, and began sobbing and lamenting to each other over our evil plight.

"It would have been better," we cried, "had we been drowned in the sea or eaten by the apes, than roasted upon a spit. As Allah lives, that is a filthy kind of death! But what can we do? Allah's will must run its course; there is no power save in Allah!"

We left the building and wandered all day about the island, searching for some cave or hiding place; but we found none, because the island was quite flat and bare. When evening fell it seemed to us the lesser of two evils to return to the palace.

We had not been there long when the black man announced his coming by a noise as of thunder; in the same way as the night before, he chose out one of the merchants whom he spitted, roasted, and ate; then he again snored like a gorged animal until the morning. At dawn he went forth again, grumbling horribly to himself and taking no notice of us at all.

By this time we had well thought over our deadly situation, so that, as soon as we were alone, we cried out: "Let us drown ourselves in the sea rather than be cooked and eaten!" We were about to put this desperate plan into execution when one of us rose, saying: "Listen to me, comrades. Would it not be better for us to kill this black man than to kill ourselves?" Then I rose in my turn and said to my friends: "If we determine to kill this giant, we must begin by constructing a raft out of the wood which litters the sea shore, so that we can escape from this cursed island when we have rid creation of our Mussulman-eating barbarian. We can make our way to some other island and there wait for a ship which will take us back to our own country. Even if the raft capsizes and we are

58

"IT IS THE ISLE OF APES," SAID THE CAPTAIN

drowned, we will have escaped roasting and avoided the unlawful act of suicide. Our death will be a martyrdom and count as such upon the Judgment Day."

"As Allah lives," cried all the other merchants, "that is an excellent plan!"

We went down to the beach and, after making our raft, loaded it with fruits and edible herbs by way of food; then we returned to the palace and waited fearfully for the coming of the black ogre.

He came with his customary thunder-clap, baying like a great mad dog, and we had to submit to the loss of the plumpest of our companions before we could put our purpose into execution. At last, when the monster was asleep and snoring like an earthquake, we took two of the iron spits and, making them red hot in the fire, laid hold of them by the cool ends and staggered with them, many to each one, towards the sleeper. With all our strength we plunged these terrible weapons into the frightful eyes of the black man and weighed upon them with our bodies until there was no doubt as to his blindness.

His pain must have been atrocious, for he gave vent to a fearful cry, which cast us all many yards away on to the floor. He bounded from the bench and lumbered about blindly with outstretched hands, yelling and attempting to find us; but we were easily able to dodge him, so that his gropings met no more than the empty air; and he soon felt his way to the door and disappeared with moans of suffering.

Feeling certain that the ogre would die of his wounds, we made our way light-heartedly towards the beach, and, after perfecting our raft, pushed it off from the shore and rowed out to sea. We were only a few yards from the shingle when we saw the blind giant run-

ning towards us, guided by a woman of his own species, in every
way more disgusting than himself. When they came to the beach,
they stood howling at us for a little while; and then, seizing upon
vast lumps of rock, bombarded the raft with them. Some of the hits
told, so that all my companions save two were drowned; but we

three who survived soon managed to paddle our craft beyond the
range of these great missiles.

As soon as we reached the open sea the wind took us and, carrying us for two days and nights, threw us upon another island, just
in time to save ourselves from death with fruit and water, and then
to climb up into a tall tree before the fall of night.

The first thing which we saw when we opened our eyes in the
morning was a vile snake, as large as the tree in which we were hid-

ing, which darted towards us with burning eyes, opening jaws as great as an oven. Suddenly the beast rose up, so that his head was on a level with the tree top, and, seizing one of my companions in his teeth, swallowed him with one movement to the shoulders and, with a second, made him disappear entirely. We heard the bones of the unfortunate man cracking in the snake's belly and thought to ourselves:

"As Allah lives, each new death which we come across seems more detestable than the others. Our joy at escaping the black man's spit needs must change to the fear of something worse! There is no help save in Allah!"

Although half unconscious with fear, we were able to climb down from the tree to eat some fruit and satisfy our thirst at a near-by stream. Afterwards we went all over the island, hunting for some more secure shelter than that of the night before, and at last found a tree so high that its upper branches appeared to be out of reach of any serpent in the world. At nightfall we climbed into the top of this and made ourselves as comfortable as we could, drawing quiet breath for the first time in many days. All at once, however, we heard a monstrous hissing and a noise of breaking branches. Before we could make a movement, the snake had seized my companion, who was sitting a little lower than I, and engulfed the first three-quarters of him with one single swallow. It was my lot to see the huge creature wrap itself around the tree and crack all the bones of my last comrade before swallowing him whole.

Though the snake now retired, I stayed in the tree without daring to move until the sun brought me warmth and confidence. My first thought was to cast myself into the sea and thus put an end to a life in which terror accumulated upon the head of terror; but, when I was half-way to the beach, my soul revolted because the spirit of man is a precious thing, and also because I had conceived a plan which I considered would finally protect me against the snake.

Having collected a large quantity of wood, I stretched myself on the ground and fixed a broad plank of it below the soles of my feet. A second and a third I secured to the outside of my thighs, a fourth in front of my belly, and a fifth and largest over my head. Thus I was surrounded on all sides by wooden bulwarks which would prove an obstacle to the snake in whatever direction he attacked me. When I had made my preparations, I stayed where I was, lying upon the ground, and delivered myself into the hands of Destiny.

At nightfall the snake came; as soon as it saw me it threw itself upon me but could not swallow me down into its belly because of my wooden protections. Therefore it turned round me, jumping up and down, to find an unguarded part, but even though it pulled me about and plagued me, it could not eat me. All night I fought, feeling its stinking breath in my face; and at dawn the terrible beast shook itself with fury and disappeared among the trees.

When I was quite sure that the snake had gone, I undid the knots which bound the planks to me and lay on the ground for many hours, suffering so throughout all my limbs that I feared that I would never recover the use of them. At last, however, I found that I could stand and began painfully to cross the island; as soon as I reached the other side and looked out to sea, I saw a ship passing swiftly with all sails set.

At sight of her I waved my arms and cried out like a madman; then I undid the stuff of my turban and, fastening it to the branch of a tree, waved it above my head as a signal of distress. Destiny willed that my despair should not pass unnoticed, the ship turned from her course and made towards the island and, in a very short time, I was rescued by the captain and his crew.

As soon as I was on board, I was given clothes to cover my nakedness and food which I devoured ravenously; but my greatest joy was a certain store of cool fresh water, from which I was allowed to drink until I was satisfied. Little by little my heart grew calm and I felt rest and well-being fall like balm upon my weary body.

I began to live again, after having looked so long upon the face of death, and thanked Allah for His mercy. Soon I became so like my old self that I looked upon my trials and misfortunes as so many bad dreams.

We made an excellent voyage before a favouring wind and came at last to the island of Salahata, where we cast anchor and the merchants went ashore to trade. As soon as they had left the ship, the captain came up to me saying: "Listen now to what I have to say to you! You are a poor man and a stranger; also, by your own account, you have suffered much; therefore I wish to aid you and help you to return to your own country, so that, when you think of me, it may be with pleasure and prayer." "O captain," I answered, "I will certainly call down blessings upon you with all my heart." "That is well," continued the good man. "Some years ago we had a passenger who was left behind on an island at which we touched. Since then there has been no news of him and we do not know whether he is dead or alive. All his goods are still in the hold and I intend to hand them over to you, that you may sell them and, keeping a commission for yourself, give me the price to carry back to the unfortunate man's family in Baghdad." "Let it be as you say, my master," I answered. "I shall ever feel gratitude to you for enabling me to earn such honest money."

The captain ordered the sailors to take the merchandise from the hold and called the ship's clerk to count and enter it, bale by bale. "To whom do these goods belong?" asked the man. "In whose name shall I write them down?" "The owner's name was Sindbad the Sailor," answered the captain, "but now you must enter it in the name of this poor passenger. Therefore ask him what that is."

"But I am Sindbad the Sailor!" I cried out in astonishment; then, looking more closely at the captain, I recognised him for the man who had forgotten me when I fell asleep on the island at the beginning of my second voyage.

Trembling with emotion, I continued: "O captain, do you not recognise me? I am indeed Sindbad the Sailor, a merchant of Baghdad. Listen to my tale! Do you not remember that it was I who went ashore upon that island many years ago and did not rejoin the ship? I ate beside a delightful stream and fell asleep, only waking to see your vessel far off upon the ocean. Many merchants in the

Mountain of Diamonds saw me and will bear witness that I am indeed Sindbad."

I had not finished my explanations when one of the merchants came aboard to make a further selection of his goods, and coming up to me, looked closely in my face. When I paused for breath he clapped his hands together in surprise, saying: "As Allah lives, none of you would believe me when I told you of the strange adventure

which happened to me one day on the Mountain of Diamonds, when I saw a man lifted from the valley to the peaks by a Roc, who had pounced upon a quarter of mutton to which the adventurer was attached. Well, this is the man! He is Sindbad the Sailor, that very generous merchant who made me a present of wonderful diamonds." So saying, my old friend embraced me as if I had been a long-lost brother.

Then the captain also looked more closely at me and suddenly recognised me as Sindbad. He took me in his arms as if I had been his son, and congratulated me on being alive, saying: "As Allah lives, my master, your adventure has been a prodigious one; but praise be to Him who has allowed us to meet again and permitted the recovery of all your goods!" With that he had the bales carried for me on to the quay and I sold them at such enormous profit that I more than made up for the time that I had lost since I purchased them.

After this we left the island of Salahata and came to the land of Sind, where all the ship's company bought and sold. In those far seas I saw so many incredible prodigies that a detailed account of them would be impossible. I saw a fish which looked like a cow and another which closely resembled an ass; also a bird which is born from a sea shell, whose little ones live ever upon the surface of the waters and do not fly over the earth. We sailed on and on until, by the permission of Allah, we came to Bassora and, staying there only a few days, hastened up stream to Baghdad.

I went to my own house in my own street and, greeting my friends, my old companions, and the folk of my family, gave great alms to the widow and orphan, because I had returned richer from my last adventure than before.

Tomorrow, my friends, if Allah wills, I will tell you the tale of my fourth voyage and you will find it more interesting than the other three. Then Sindbad the Sailor gave Sindbad the Porter a hundred pieces of gold, as he had done on the days which went before, and invited him to return next morning.

Next day the porter returned and, when the usual feast was finished, heard Sindbad the Sailor tell of:

THE FOURTH VOYAGE

THE DELIGHTFUL PLEASURES
of my life in Baghdad could not make me forget my voyages; though
my memories did not dwell upon the hardships and the dangers
which had been my lot. My traitor soul only showed me the advantageous side of travelling in far countries, so that at last I could
resist her whisperings no longer and, leaving my house and great
possessions, provided myself with a greater quantity of precious
merchandise than I had ever carried before and had it conveyed to
Bassora. There I embarked upon a great ship in company with some
of the best known merchants of the city.

We made excellent time across the seas, trading to great profit
from island to island and from land to land, until one day, when we
were in mid-ocean, the captain suddenly gave the order to anchor,
crying: "We are lost beyond all hope!" A great wind raised all the
sea about us and, hurling heavy seas against the ship, broke it to

pieces and washed all who were aboard into the gulfs of the water.

Thanks to Allah, I found a plank in the depths and, clinging to it with hands and feet, tossed hither and thither for half a day with certain other of the merchants who had managed to reach it also. Rowing with our hands and feet and helped by wind and current, we were thrown, more dead than alive with cold and terror, upon the beach of an island.

We lay as we were upon the sand all night, but in the morning we were able to rise and make our way into the interior, where we saw a building among the trees.

As we drew nearer, a crowd of naked black men streamed from the door of this building; without saying a word they surrounded us and led us into a mighty hall where a king was sitting upon a high throne.

This monarch bade us be seated and then had trays brought covered with such meats as we had never seen in our lives before. Their appearance did not excite my appetite but my companions ate greedily because of the hunger which we had suffered since our shipwreck. Though I did not know it at the time, my abstention saved my life.

After the first few mouthfuls, the other merchants were seized with such a fit of gluttony that they went on swallowing and swallowing for many hours all that was put before them, with mad gestures and strange snuffling sounds. While they still continued to guzzle, the naked men fetched a vase filled with a kind of ointment with which they anointed the bodies of all the guests who were feeding heartily. The effect upon the bellies of my friends was extraordinary; I saw them, little by little, grow larger in all directions, until the stomach of each was swollen to the size of a great waterskin. Their appetites increased in proportion, so that they went on eating and I was aghast to see that my friends were never filled.

The sight was so terrifying that I would touch nothing and refused to be anointed; this sobriety on my part was a lucky thing, for I soon discovered that these naked men were eaters of human flesh and used these strange ways of fattening those who fell into their hands and making their flesh more tender and juicy. The king was an ogre who ate every day a roasted stranger prepared by the method which I have described, but the naked men preferred their abominable diet raw, just as it was, without cooking or seasoning of any kind.

At this terrible discovery my fear for myself and my friends knew no bounds, especially when I noticed that the more their bellies swelled the less their intelligence became, until they ate themselves at last into a state of mere brutishness and, when they had become in no way different from slaughter cattle, were put in charge of a herdsman, who took them out every day to feed upon the meadows.

I myself was worn to a shadow with hunger and fear, and the flesh became dry upon my bones, so that the natives took no notice of me and forgot all about me, realising that I was unworthy to be roasted or even grilled for their king.

As the black islanders did not watch me, I was able one day to leave the building in which they lived and make off across the island. As I went I met the herdsman in charge of my unfortunate friends and hastened to hide myself in the tall grass, dodging from tuft to tuft until I had passed them, in order not to be tortured by a sight of their distressing condition.

I walked straight ahead all night, fear of these cannibals having driven away all desire for sleep; and, with only such time as was necessary to take an occasional meal of herbs, I journeyed on towards the unknown for six whole days and nights.

On the morning of the eighth day I came to the opposite side of the island and saw men like myself, white and clothed, gathering pepper from the trees which covered that spot. When they saw me they gathered round me, speaking my own language which I had not heard for so long. In answer to their questions, I told them that I was a poor stranger and related the story of my misfortunes. They were exceedingly astonished by what they heard and, after congratulating me on my escape, offered me food and drink, let me sleep for an hour, and then took me down with them into their ship that they might carry me over and present me to their king, who lived in a neighbouring island.

I found the capital, when we came to it, largely populated, abounding in the excellent things of life, rich in markets, and good shops, transpierced by beautiful roads, where a multitude of horsemen galloped up and down, with neither saddle nor spurs, upon horses of a wonderful breed. When I was presented to the king, I did not omit, after respectful greetings, to tell him of my astonishment on seeing men riding bare-backed. "O my master and lord," I said, "why do people not use saddles here? They are excellent things and make a man much more the master of his horse."

The king was astonished and asked me: "What thing is this saddle? We have never seen one in all our life." I answered: "Will you allow me to make you one, that you may find out how comfortable and useful a thing it is?"

The king accepted my offer, so I found out a clever carpenter and made him prepare, under my own eyes, a wooden saddle according to my specifications. As soon as it was finished, I provided the wooden basis with a padding of linen and leather, ornamenting it all about with gold embroidery and tassels of different colours.

Then I taught a certain blacksmith how to make a bit and a pair of spurs and, because I did not leave him for a moment, he performed his task admirably.

When all was perfect, I chose out the handsomest horse from the king's stables, saddled and bridled it, and equipped it splendidly with such ornaments as long skirts, tassels of silk and gold, and blue tufts about the collar. Then I led it to the presence of the king, who had

been impatiently waiting the result of my labours for several days.

The king mounted at once and felt himself so satisfied with the easy mastery which he now had over his horse, that he gave me sumptuous presents and large sums of money.

No sooner had the grand-wazir seen my saddle and realised what an improvement it was upon the old way of riding, than he begged me to make him one like it. I hastened to oblige him; and then all the notables and high dignitaries of the kingdom asked and received saddles in their turn, rewarding me with such presents that I soon became the richest and most respected man in the city.

I was soon a fast friend of the king and one day, while I was with him, he turned to me, saying: "You know that I love you, Sindbad; you have become like one of my own people in my palace, so that I cannot do without you or tolerate the idea that you will some day leave us; therefore I wish to ask you a favour which I hope you will not refuse." "You have but to order, O king," I answered, "your power over me is made strong by gratitude for all the benefits I have received since my arrival in your pleasant kingdom." "Then," continued the king, "I wish you to marry a very beautiful woman of the court. She is both rich and talented, and I trust she will be able to persuade you to stay in our city and palace until the end of your days. Do not refuse me this, O Sindbad."

I lowered my eyes in confusion and did not know what to answer. "Why do you not speak, my child?" asked the king; and I stammered out: "O prince of time, the matter is in your hands; I am your slave." At once he sent for the kadi and witnesses, and married me in that same hour to a noble woman of distinguished family. She was extremely rich, owning goods, buildings, and lands, beside her own considerable beauty. The king also gave me a furnished palace with servants, with men slaves and women slaves, and a following which was truly royal.

I lived in the calmness of supreme joy for many months after my marriage and ever nourished the secret hope of escaping from that city and returning to Baghdad with my wife; for we loved each other and the accord between us was marvellous. But when Destiny proposes a thing no human power can turn that thing aside. Also what man may know the future? Alas, I was soon to learn yet again

EXTREMELY RICH, AND A CONSIDERABLE BEAUTY

that all of our projects are but child's play in the eyes of Fate.

One day my neighbour's wife died, for Allah had willed it so; and, as he was my friend, I went to him and tried to console him, saying: "Do not grieve more than is lawful, O my neighbour; Allah will soon make up to you for your loss by giving you an even better wife. May He prolong your days, my friend!" The man seemed stupefied by my words; he raised his head, saying: "How can you wish me a long life, when you know that I have but an hour to live?" Astounded in my turn, I said: "Why do you speak in that way? What gloomy presentiments are these? Thanks be to Allah, you are in perfect health and nothing threatens you; surely you do not mean that you are going to kill yourself?" He answered: "Ah, now I see that you do not know the customs of our country. It is a rule here that every husband must be buried alive with his dead wife and every wife buried alive with her dead husband. The law is inviolable; and in an hour's time I shall be committed to the earth with the body of my wife. Every man, and even the king, must conform to this custom of our ancestors."

At these words I cried: "As Allah lives, the custom is detestable; I never could find it in my heart to abide by it."

While we were speaking, the friends and relations of my neighbour came in and began to console him as best they might for his own and his wife's death. Then the funeral went forward; the woman's body was placed in an open coffin, dressed in her most beautiful garments and wearing the chief of her jewels; a procession was formed with the husband at the head, walking behind the coffin; and we all proceeded with slow steps towards the place of burial.

We came outside the city to a mountain overlooking the sea; in a certain part of it I saw a kind of immense well, the stone cover of

which was speedily lifted. First the coffin was let down and then my
friend was seized and, without offering any resistance, allowed himself to be lowered into the well by a long rope to which was also
attached a large jar of water and seven loaves. Then the stone cover
was replaced upon the well and we all returned whence we had come.

I had assisted at this ceremony, sick with fear and thinking: "This
is more terrible than anything I have yet seen." No sooner did I
reach the palace, than I ran to the king, saying: "My master, I have
travelled through many lands, but I have never heard of so barbarous
an institution as your custom of burying a husband alive with his
dead wife. I should like to know, O king of time, if a stranger is
equally amenable to this law." "Certainly he is," answered the
king, "he must be buried alive with his wife."

At this answer I felt as if my gall-bladder would break against my
liver; half mad with terror, I ran to my own house, fearing lest my
wife might have died in my absence. When I found her in the best
of health, I tried to console myself, saying: "Do not be afraid, O
Sindbad; you are certain to be the first to die, therefore you will
never be buried alive." But this consolation was vain; for in a short
while my wife fell ill and, after lying upon her bed for certain days,
rendered her soul to Allah in spite of all the cares with which I surrounded her.

My grief and horror knew no bounds, for I considered it as bad
to be buried alive as to be eaten by cannibals. I could have no doubt
about my fate when the king came to visit me and condoled with
me over my approaching end. He was so fond of me that he insisted
on being present with all his court at my burial, and himself walked
beside me when I headed the procession behind the coffin in which
my dead wife lay, covered with jewels and ornaments.

When we came to the mountain which overlooked the sea, the well was opened and the body of my wife let down; then all who had come with me clustered round to say farewell. I tried to move the heart of the king by weeping and crying: "I am a stranger and it is not just that I should have to suffer by your law. I have a living wife in my own country and children who have need of me."

The people took no notice of my sobs and lamentations but fixed ropes under my arms and, tying a jar of water and the seven customary loaves to my back, lowered me into the well. When I had reached the bottom of it, they cried down to me: "Unfasten yourself, that we may pull up the ropes!" This I was unwilling to do, but rather kept on pulling upon the cord as a sign that they should haul me up again. Therefore they let go of the ropes, reclosed the mouth of the well with the great stone and went their way, followed by my pitiable cries.

At once the stench of this fearful underground place made me stop my nose, but it did not prevent me from using the light which filtered from above to inspect this mortuary cave, which I found to be filled with old and new bodies. It was very high and stretched further than my eye could reach. I fell to the earth weeping and crying: "You deserve this fate, O Sindbad of the unfilled soul! What need was there for you to marry in this city? Why did you not die in the valley of diamonds? Why did you not perish at the teeth of the cannibals? Would that it had pleased Allah to drown you in one of your shipwrecks rather than reserve you for so terrible a death!" I beat myself in the face and the stomach with my fists; but at last, feeling the effects of both hunger and thirst and being determined not to die out of hand, unfastened the loaves and the water from the rope and ate and drank sparingly.

I lived in this way for several days, growing gradually used to the foul odour of the cave and sleeping at night upon a space of earth which I had taken care to clear of bones. The time came when I had neither bread nor water; I had just recited the act of faith in absolute despair and shut my eyes before the approach of death, when the cover was removed above my head and a dead man was let down in his coffin, accompanied by his wife with seven loaves and a jar of water.

I waited until the men above had covered the opening again and then noiselessly possessing myself of a great bone from one of the dead, threw myself upon the woman and brought my weapon down upon her head; I gave her a second and a third blow to make sure that she was dead and then took the seven loaves and the water jar, which kept me alive for several further days.

At the end of that time the covering was again removed and a dead woman was let down with her husband. Life is dear, so I killed the man and took his bread and water. In this way I lived for a long time, killing each new person who was buried and stealing their provisions.

One day, as I was sleeping in my ordinary place, I was aroused by an unaccustomed noise as of living breath and hurrying feet. I rose and, taking my bone, followed the noise until I could just distinguish some heavily breathing object fleeing away from me. I followed this escaping shadow for a long time, running behind it in the dark, stumbling over the bones of the dead, until suddenly I saw in front of me something like a luminous star which shone and faded out by turns. As I went on towards it, this light grew larger; but I dared not believe that it portended any way of escape, but thought rather that it was a second shaft by which the dead and living were let down. All at once, however, the form in front of me, which I could now see to belong to some animal, bounded through the light and disappeared; then, to my great joy, I realised that I had come upon a hole burrowed by savage beasts, attracted by the bodies in the cave. I followed where the animal had gone before and soon found myself in the open air, beneath the sky of heaven.

I fell upon my knees and thanked the Highest with all my heart for my salvation and, by my prayers, brought peace to my soul. Then I looked about me and saw that I was at the foot of a mountain beside the sea and that this mountain was so steep and jagged that there could be no communication between the place I was in and the city. Not wishing to die of hunger, I returned to the cave and brought out food and water, which I ate and drank in the sunlight with better appetite than I had ever used in the charnel cavern.

I went on living this way, returning every day to the cave for food and water, which I obtained by dashing out the brains of those who were buried alive. Also the idea came to me of collecting from the dead all their jewellery, diamonds, bracelets, collars, pearls, rubies, engraved metals, rich garments, and ornaments of gold and silver. These things I hoarded on the sea shore in the hope that some day I might be able to escape with them; and, that all should be ready, made them up into strong bundles with the garments of the men and women in the cavern.

I was sitting one day, lost in dreams of my adventures and my present state, when I saw a ship passing near in; I rose hastily, and undoing the stuff of my turban, made vigorous signs with it, as I ran up and down the sand. Thanks be to Allah, the men in the ship saw my signal and sent ashore a boat which took me and all my packages aboard.

When I came on deck, the captain approached me, saying: "Who are you, and how did you come upon that mountain on which, during all the years that I have sailed these seas, I have never seen anything but savage beasts and birds of prey?" "O master," I answered, "I am a poor merchant, stranger to these lands. The great ship in which I voyaged was lost with all her company except myself, who by courage and endurance succeeded in reaching this coast, with all my merchandise, on a large plank which I gripped as the boat went down. As you see, Allah saved me from dying of hunger and thirst." This I said to the captain, being very careful not to tell him of my marriage and burial, lest there should be some aboard who belonged to that barbarous city.

When I had finished explaining myself to the captain, I took a rich jewel from one of my bales and offered it to him, that he might be propitious to me during the voyage. To my great surprise, however, he showed a most rare disinterestedness and refused my payment, saying kindly: "It is not my custom to ask for payment when I do a good deed. You are not the first whom I have taken up alive out of the sea; I have served many a wrecked mariner and carried him to his own country, for Allah's sake, giving him food, water, and clothes, and also a little something for the expenses of his further journey. For Allah's sake men should behave to men as men."

I thanked the captain and wished him a long life; after which he set all sail and proceeded with his voyage.

We had fair weather from island to island and from sea to sea, so that I could lie pleasantly for hours together recalling my adventures and asking myself whether all my dangers and escapes had not been dreams. Sometimes, however, a memory of my sojourn underground with my dead wife came back to me and I would go half mad.

SINDBAD BURIED IN THE CAVE

At last, by the grace of Allah, we came safely to Bassora where we stayed a few days and then proceeded up the river to Baghdad.

I hurried to my own house in my own street, loaded with riches, and presented myself before my friends and the men and women of my family, who rejoiced over my return with great festivity and congratulated me on my safety. When I had given bounteous alms to the poor, the widow, and the orphan, and large presents to my friends and acquaintances, I shut my treasure in presses and gave myself up to every kind of pleasure and diversion in the company of gracious people.

But all that I have told you is nothing to that which I will tell you tomorrow, if Allah wills.

So spoke Sindbad on that day; and afterwards gave a hundred pieces of gold to the porter and invited him to dine that night in company with the great folk who were present. When the feast was over, all the guests returned marvelling to their own homes.

Sindbad the Porter returned to his own home, where he dreamed all night of the story he had heard. When he returned to the house of Sindbad the Sailor, his soul was still sick with the thought of how his friend had been buried alive. Yet, as the cloth was already laid, he took his place with the others to eat and drink and thank Allah therefor. At length silence fell upon all and Sindbad the Sailor related:

THE FIFTH VOYAGE

AFTER MY FOURTH VOYAGE

I lived so pleasantly, so joyfully, that I soon forgot my past sufferings and remembered only the great profit which my extraordinary adventures had gained for me. You will not be surprised, then, to hear that I soon obeyed the promptings of my soul when she incited me to further travel among the lands of men.

I bought a quantity of that merchandise which I knew by experience would meet with a ready sale at high prices and, after it had been packed in bales, took it down stream with me to Bassora.

Walking on the quay there, I saw a new-built ship of great size, which pleased me so much that I bought her out of hand. I hired an experienced captain and a sturdy crew; and then had my bales of merchandise carried on board by the slaves whom I was taking with me to serve me on the voyage and, lastly, accepted as passengers certain honest merchants who paid their money upon the spot. Being this time master of the ship, I felt that I would be able to assist the captain with my knowledge of the sea.

We set sail light-heartedly from Bassora and met favourable winds and a calm sea. After buying and selling at various ports of call, we came one day to an uninhabited island whose sole building appeared to be a large white dome. This I recognised as a Roc's egg, but unfortunately I said nothing about it to my passengers; so that, when they went ashore, they found no better employment than to throw great stones at the shell of the egg. When the surface was broken, a liquid substance flowed forth and this, to their great surprise, was followed by one of the legs of the small Roc. The merchants went on with their work of destruction and, after killing the young bird, cut it in pieces and returned on board to tell me of their adventure. I was stricken with fear on hearing what they had done and cried: "We are lost! The father and mother will be here soon and they will destroy us; we must get away as quickly as we can!"

I gave immediate orders for the sails to be set and we made for the open sea.

As we hurried away from the island the merchants set to work to cook the pieces of the bird; but they had hardly begun to eat when

87

we perceived two great clouds hiding the sun. These drew nearer and we saw that they were two gigantic Rocs; we heard the beating of their wings and their cries which were more terrible than thunder. When they were high above our heads we saw, moreover, that each carried in its talons a rock larger than our vessel.

Realising the kind of vengeance which they meant to take, we gave ourselves up for lost. Soon one of the birds let its missile fall directly above the boat; but the captain, with a dexterous turn of the tiller, threw us from our course. The mighty stone just missed us and opened up so great a well in the sea that we could see the bottom, and we were tossed up and down like a cork upon the consequent waves. Before these had subsided, the second bird let fall its rock, which struck our stern and, breaking the tiller into twenty pieces, swamped half of the vessel in the sea. Those of us who were not crushed to pieces were thrown into the water and dragged down by the waves.

I was able to rise to the surface through the desperate efforts which I made to save my life and, by good luck, managed to clamber on to one of the timbers of the lost ship. Sitting astride this I paddled with my feet and, by the aid of wind and current, reached an island, just as I was about to render my last breath to its Giver, from weariness, hunger, and thirst. I threw myself upon the beach and lay there for an hour until my heart had ceased its inordinate beating and strength had a little returned to me. Then I rose and began to make an examination of the island.

This time I did not have to go far, for Fate had carried me to a very garden of Paradise.

On all sides, before my delighted eyes, were trees with golden fruit, cold silver streams, a thousand wings of birds, and close carpets of scented flowers. I did not delay to eat the fruits, drink the water, and breathe in the refreshment of the flowers.

I stayed where I was, resting from my exertions until the evening; but when night fell and I knew myself alone upon the island among those trees, I became suddenly afraid, although beauty and peace surrounded me on every side. Therefore I could hardly sleep and, when I dozed, was visited by fearful nightmares. Dawn brought me a certain measure of tranquillity, so I rose and began to extend my exploration of the island. I soon came to a large pool into which dropped the waters of a fall and saw, sitting upon its edge, an old man, clothed in a great cloak of sewn leaves. "This is some ship-wrecked sailor like myself," I thought.

I went up to the old man and wished him peace; but he only answered by signs. "How come you to be in this place, O venerable sheikh?" I asked; but he only shook his head sadly and signed with his hand, as much as to say: "I beg you to take me upon your shoulders and carry me across the stream, for I would pluck the fruits upon the other side." "Sindbad," I said to myself, "if you help this old man you will be doing a good deed." So I bent down and took him upon my shoulders, crossing his legs upon my chest, while he clasped my neck with his thighs and my head with his arms. I carried him across the stream to the spot which he had indicated and then bent down again, saying: "Alight gently, O venerable stranger"; but he did not move, rather he pressed his thighs more tightly round my neck and weighed down upon my shoulders with all his weight.

I was surprised at this and looked more carefully at his legs, which I then saw to be black and rough and furry like the skin of a buffalo. A great fear took me and I tried to throw the old man to the earth, but he replied by pressing my throat until I was half strangled and dark shadows began to appear before my eyes. I made a last effort to dislodge my persecutor and then fell senseless to the ground.

When I came to myself, I found the old man still crouched on my shoulders, with this difference only, that he had slightly opened his legs to let the air return to my body. As soon as he saw that I was again breathing, he kicked me in the stomach until I got up, and then hunched down further upon my neck and signed to me, with one of his hands, to walk beneath the trees. When I did so, he leisurely plucked the fine fruits and ate them; each time I stopped against his will or went too fast he kicked me violently until I did as he wished. All that day he stayed upon my shoulders and I was no better than a beast of burden; and at night he made me lie down with him so that he could sleep without leaving his position. In the morning he woke me with a kick in the belly and made me carry him as before.

For the whole of the next day and night he stayed immovable upon my back, doing all his liquid and solid needs upon me, and urging me to my work with fist and feet.

I had never suffered such humiliation of spirit or discomfort of body as I experienced in the service of that old man, who was as strong as a youth and as cruel as a donkey-driver; and yet I could find no way to get rid of him. I trudged up and down, cursing the virtuous impulse which had led me to help the sinister old man and begging for death rather than a continuance of this slavery.

One day, after weeks of servitude, I was carrying my rider under certain trees below which lay great gourds, and the idea came to me to use a gourd as a receptacle for wine. Picking up one of the largest, which was quite dry, I thoroughly emptied and cleaned it. Then I squeezed the grapes of a prolific vine into it and, carefully stopping

FATHER ROC & MOTHER ROC, TERRIBLE IN VENGEANCE

the opening which I had cut, left it in the sun; so that, in a few days, it was filled with pure wine. When the fermentation had ceased I drank enough to increase my strength and help me to bear the weight of my burden, but not enough to make me drunk. Yet I felt a new man and very gay; for the first time, I began to jump from side to side with my rider, whose weight I did not feel, and went dancing and singing through the trees. I even clapped my hands in praise of my own dancing and made the glades re-echo with my peals of laughter.

When the old man saw me in this unaccustomed state and real-ised that my strength was doubled so that I carried him without fatigue, he signed to me to pass him the gourd. I did not wish to comply with this request, but my fear of the old man was too great for me to refuse. He took the gourd from my hand and, carrying it to his lips, took first a tentative taste and then drank it down to the last drop and threw the gourd far off among the trees.

Soon the wine began to work in his brain, for he had taken quite enough to make him drunk; first he danced and jigged on my shoul-ders and then half collapsed with slack muscles, bending over to right and left and keeping his seat with difficulty.

Feeling that I was not clasped as strongly as usual, I unfastened his legs from my neck with a rapid movement and then, by an urge of my shoulders, threw the old man to the ground some feet away from me, where he lay without movement. Without more ado, I picked up a great rock from among the trees and, throwing myself upon my tormentor, smashed his skull to pieces and mingled his blood with his flesh. Thus he died; may Allah have no compassion upon his soul!

When I saw the corpse, my spirit grew as light as my body and I ran joyfully down to the sea shore, where Destiny willed I should find a party of sailors who had disembarked from an anchored ship to hunt for water and fruit. They were astonished to see me and clustered round, asking questions. I told them what had happened to me both on sea and land: that is to say, that I had been wrecked and afterwards reduced to bestial servitude by the old man whom I had eventually killed.

On hearing my tale, the sailors cried: "It is a matter of marvel that you escaped from that old man; he is known to all mariners as the Old Man of the Sea and you are the first whom he has not strangled with his thighs. Praise be to Allah that He has delivered you!"

They took me to their ship, where the captain received me kindly and gave me clothes to cover my nakedness. When he had heard my story he also congratulated me, and then set sail.

After many days and nights at sea we entered the port of a well-built city upon a certain coast. I soon learned that it was called the City of Apes because of the prodigious quantity of those beasts living in the trees which surrounded it.

I disembarked with one of the merchants who was on board, wishing to see if I could find some employment in the city. As we were walking away from the harbour, the merchant, who had become very friendly towards me, gave me a linen bag, saying: "Fill this with pebbles and go join the crowd of people whom you will see issuing from the gates. Act in every way as they act and you will earn more than enough money for your livelihood."

Following his instructions, I filled the bag with pebbles and joined myself to a troop which I saw come out from the city gates, each carrying a bag similar to my own. My friend, the merchant, recommended me in the highest terms to these people, saying: "Here is a poor stranger; if you will teach him to earn his daily bread, Allah will reward you."

After walking for some time, we came to a deep valley, covered with trees so tall that no man might essay to climb them; and the branches of these were heavy with apes and a large thick-skinned fruit called cocoa-nuts.

We halted below the trees and my companions, setting their bags on the ground, began to bombard the apes with pebbles; and I did the like. The animals were excited to fury and answered each stone by throwing down a cocoa-nut, so that we gathered a vast quantity of this fruit and put it into our bags. When they were full we put them on our shoulders and returned to the city, where my friend the merchant took back the sack which he had given me and gave me the value of its contents in silver. I went out every day with the cocoa-nut hunters and sold my booty in the city; thus, before long, I saved a considerable sum of money, which I increased by shrewd sale and exchange till it became enough to pay my passage to the Sea of Pearls.

I took a great quantity of cocoa-nuts with me, which I exchanged among the islands for pepper and cinnamon; these last two commodities I sold so advantageously during the rest of my journey that, when at last I came to the Sea of Pearls, I was able to take divers into my service.

My luck never once deserted me in the pearl fishing and it was not long before I had collected an immense fortune. Then, being unwilling to put off my return any longer, I bought a quantity of the best aloe-wood, such as abounds in these idolatrous seas, and took a boat which brought me safely to Bassora. When I reached

Baghdad, I ran to my own house in my own street, where I was joyfully received by my friends and relations.

As I had returned richer than I had ever been before, I spread fortunate ease about me by making judicious presents to those who needed them. I myself settled down to a life of perfect peace and happiness.

Dine with me tonight, my friends, and tomorrow you shall hear of my sixth voyage which turned out so astonishing that, in hearing of it, you will forget all the adventures I have yet told you.

When Sindbad the Sailor had made an end of the account of his fifth journey, he gave a hundred gold pieces to the porter, who, after feasting, departed with the other marvelling guests. Next day Sindbad told the same company the tale of:

THE SIXTH VOYAGE

COMPANIONS AND DEAR guests, I was sitting one day taking the air before my door and feeling as happy as I had ever felt, when I saw a group of merchants passing in the street who had every appearance of returned travellers. This sight recalled to me how joyful a thing it is to return from journeying, to see the birth land after far voyage, and the thought made me long to travel again. I equipped myself with merchandise of price, suitable for the sea, and left the city of Baghdad for Bassora. There I found a great ship filled with merchants and notables as well provided with goods for trading as myself; so I had my bales carried on board and soon we peacefully set sail from Bassora.

We sailed from place to place and from city to city buying and selling and rejoicing in the new sights which met our gaze. But one day, as we were lying on the deck with a feeling of perfect safety, we heard despairing cries and, looking up, saw that they were uttered by the captain, who also threw his turban far away from him and, beating himself on the face, pulled out handfuls of his beard.

We clustered round him, asking what the matter was, and he answered: "All good folk here assembled, learn that we have been driven from the seas we knew into an unknown ocean where we shall surely perish, unless Allah sends something to save us. Let us pray to Him!"

So saying the captain climbed the mast and was about to trim the sails, when a great wind rose and, striking us full in the face, broke our rudder to pieces just as we were passing a high mountain. The captain swarmed down the mast, crying: "There is no power or might save in Allah! None can arrest the force of Destiny! My friends, we are altogether lost!"

While the passengers were weeping and saying farewell to each other, the sea rose in her fury and broke our vessel into fragments against the mountain of which I have spoken. We were all thrown into the water, where some were drowned and others, among whom was myself, were able to save themselves by clinging to the lower crags.

Now this mountain rose straight up from the strand of a large island, the beaches of which were covered with the remains of wrecked ships and every kind of jetsam. The place where we landed was strewn with a multitude of bales from which rich merchandise and costly ornaments had escaped.

I walked among these scattered treasures and soon found a little river of fresh water which, instead of flowing into the sea, as do all other rivers, came from a cleft in the mountain and, running inland, at last plunged into a cave at the foot of it and disappeared.

Nor was that all; the banks of this stream were thick underfoot with rubies and other coloured precious stones, and all crumbling

"ALL THESE RICHES WERE USELESS TO MAN"

with diamonds and pieces of gold and silver. Also its bed was littered with gems beyond price, instead of pebbles; and the whole
region, beneath and beside the water, blazed with the reflected light
of so much riches that the eyes of the beholder were dazzled. Chinese and Comarin aloes of the first quality grew about the water.
In this island there was a stream of raw liquid amber, of the colour
of tar, which flowed down to the sea shore, being melted to the
consistency of boiling wax by the rays of the sun. Great fish would
come out of the sea and drink greedily of this substance, which
heated their bellies, so that after a certain time they would vomit
upon the surface of the water. There it became hard and changed
both its nature and colour; at last it was carried back to the beach
in the form of ambergris, which scented the whole island. The
liquid amber, which the fish did not swallow, also spread a perfume
of musk about the shore.

All these riches were useless to man because none might touch
upon that island and leave it alive, seeing that every ship which
came near was dashed to pieces by the force of the waves.

Those of us who had been saved remained in sorrowful case upon
the beach, desolate in the middle of great wealth and starving among
the material for many feasts. Such food as we had we scrupulously
divided; but my companions, who were not used like myself to the
horrors of starvation, ate their shares in one or two meals and began
to die off in a few days. I was more careful, eating sparsely and only
once a day. Also I had found a separate supply of provision of which
I said nothing to my friends.

We who lived washed those who died and, wrapping them in
shrouds made up of the rich fabrics which strewed the shore, buried
them in the sand. To add to the hardships of the survivors, a sick-

ness of the belly broke out among us caused by the moist air of the sea. All but myself of those who had not starved died of it, and I dug with my own hands a grave for the last of my companions.

In spite of my prudent abstention, very little of my food remained; so, seeing that death was not far off, I wept and cried aloud: "Ah, why did you not die while there remained comrades who would have washed you and given you to the earth? There is no power or might save in Allah!" Then I began to bite the hands of my despair.

I rose and dug a deep grave for myself, saying: "When I feel that my last moment is at hand, I will drag myself here and die in my grave; for surely the wind will bury me with sand." As I was engaged in this work, I cursed myself bitterly for my foolishness in voyaging again after having learned five times that death lies in wait for the wanderer. "How many times did you repent and begin again?" I said to myself. "Had you not enough riches laid by in Baghdad to suffice for the most reckless expenditure throughout two lifetimes?"

To these thoughts succeeded a more practical one, suggested by the appearance of the river. "As Allah lives," I thought, "this stream must have both a beginning and an end; now, I see the beginning but the end is hidden from me. The water flows below the mountain, therefore I will wager that it comes out the other side in one fashion or another. If that is so, my only hope of escape is to construct some kind of a vessel which will bear me down the current of the stream and through its subterranean course. If such is my destiny, I will find a way of safety beyond; if I die it will be no worse than the starvation which waits me here."

A little cheered by this desperate chance, I rose and began to put my plan into execution. I collected the larger branches of the Chinese and Comarin aloes and bound them together with cords. Using this as a foundation, I built a raft with ships' planks and furnishings which was nearly but not quite as broad as the river. Then I loaded the raft with some large sacks of emeralds, pearls, and other stones, choosing always the biggest from the heaps which surrounded me. I also placed on board some bales of chosen ambergris and the rest of my provisions. When the craft balanced well, I went on board, carrying two planks by way of oars, and confided myself to Allah, remembering these words of the poet:

> Out of the country of oppression
> 　Depart and save your spirit whole;
> 　There are a thousand lands and but one soul,
> So leave the land and keep the soul's possession.

> Nothing unwritten shall surprise you,
> 　Nothing which has not been for ages;
> 　So hurry not for counsel to the sages,
> But stay at home and let your soul advise you.

My raft was hurried by the current under the arch of the cave, and at once began to bang against the sides violently; while my head often came into contact with a rocky roof which I could not see because of the sudden darkness. Very soon I wished that I could return to the sands of my starvation, but the current grew stronger and stronger as I descended the underground river and the course of it went sometimes wide and sometimes narrow so that the moving shadows thickened about me and confused my eyes. Leaving go of my useless oars I threw myself flat down upon the raft to save my head from being crushed by any projection and, worn out by fear and exhaustion, fell into a deep sleep.

This sleep or swoon of mine seemed to last for more than a year; when I came to myself I was in full daylight and, opening my eyes, saw that I was lying upon the grass in a vast tract of meadow land and that my raft was fastened by the side of a river. About me were many Indians and Abyssinians.

When these men saw that I was awake they began to speak to me, but I did not understand their language and so could not answer them. I thought I was in a dream until a man came towards me who wished me peace in pure Arabic, saying: "Who are you and where have you come from and why have you journeyed to our country? We are farmers who, arriving to water our fields and plantations in this place, saw you come down stream asleep upon a raft which we stopped and fastened here by the bank, while we laid you upon the grass to have your slumber out. We wished you to wake yourself so that you should not be afraid. Tell us by what strange adventure you have come to this place." "As Allah lives, my master," I answered, "first give me something to eat, for I am starving. Then ask me as many questions as you like." The man hastened to bring me food and I ate until I was satisfied and strengthened. Feeling my soul come back to its body, I thanked Allah and congratulated myself upon my escape from the underground river. Then I told the men who surrounded me the whole story of my adventures on the island.

They marvelled much at what they heard and began talking together in their unknown tongue; and he who spoke Arabic translated their thoughts to me as he had translated my tale to them. It appeared that they wished to conduct me to their king that he might hear my adventures for himself; when I gladly consented, they formed a procession and led me to the city, carrying with them my

THE ARRIVAL AT SERENDIB

raft, just as it was, loaded with ambergris and with sacks of jewels.

The king kindly received me and, at his request, I gave a complete recital of all that had happened to me, without omitting a single detail. But it would be useless to repeat it in this place.

The king of Serendib, for such was the name of the island, congratulated me heartily upon having come alive out of such perils; and, in return, I hastened to open my bales and sacks in his presence that he might see that there was profit attached to strange and fantastic voyaging.

The king admired my collection, for he was very learned in the matter of precious stones; and was pleased to accept samples which I offered him of every kind of jewel, together with a few large pearls and pure ingots of gold and silver. In recognition of my generosity, he loaded me with honours and gave me lodging in his own palace, so that from that day I was his friend and the friend of the chief nobles in the island. They asked me about my own country and I described it to them; then I questioned them about theirs and received some interesting answers. I learned that the island of Serendib was twenty-four parasangs long by twenty-four wide; that it held the highest mountain in the whole world, on which our father Adam had lived for certain of his days; and that it was rich in pearls and precious stones (though not so fine as mine) and many cocoanut palms.

One day the king of Serendib questioned me concerning the internal affairs of Baghdad and the government of the khalifat, Haroun Al-Rachid; I told him how just and benevolent our ruler was and laid considerable stress upon his virtues and excellent qualities. The king of Serendib marvelled at what I told him, and said: "I see that the khalifat is versed in wisdom and the true art of government. I have conceived an affection for him through the account which you have given me; therefore I am very anxious to send him some present worthy of himself, and appoint you the bearer of it." "I am entirely at your orders, my master," I answered. "I swear that I will faithfully remit your gift to the khalifat and that he will be enchanted by it. I will also tell him that you are a good friend and that he may count on your alliance."

Without delay the king gave orders to his chamberlains. The present which he sent by me to Haroun Al-Rachid consisted of: a large jar half a foot high and a finger thick, carved from a single ruby of perfect colour, filled with round white pearls as large as nuts; a carpet made from the skin of a gigantic serpent with scales each as large as a dinar and having this virtue, that whatsoever sick man lay down upon it should be healed; two hundred balls of camphor, in its purest state each as large as a pistachio; two elephant's tusks twelve cubits long and two cubits round the base; and lastly, a beautiful girl of Serendib, smothered in rich jewellery.

At the same time the king gave me a letter for the Commander of the Faithful, saying: "Make my excuses to the khalifat for sending so small a present and tell him that I love him with all my heart. . . . Yet, Sindbad, if you would rather stay in our kingdom, you shall be in everything our favourite and we will send another messenger to Baghdad instead of you." "As Allah lives, O king of time," I cried, "your generosity is a royal generosity; my spirit bows beneath your gifts, but there is a boat just starting for Bassora and I am very anxious to go aboard her and see my friends, my children, and my native land once more."

The king, who did not wish to constrain me against my will, at once sent for the captain of the ship and the merchants who would sail with me and gave me into their safe keeping with a thousand recommendations, paying my passage money himself, and presenting me with many precious gifts, which I still keep in memory of him.

After saying farewell to the king and to all the friends whom I had made in that delightful island, I set sail and at last came, through the mercy of Allah, safely to Bassora and thence to Baghdad. The first thing I did on landing was to hasten to the palace, where I was granted a reception by the Prince of Believers. I kissed the earth between his hands and, giving him the letter and present with which I had been intrusted, told him all my adventures from beginning to end.

When the khalifat had read the letter from the king of Serendib and examined the presents, he asked me if the monarch, who had sent them, was really as rich as these things seemed to imply. "O Commander of the Faithful," I answered, "I can witness that the king of Serendib does not exaggerate, and further that he adds to his wealth both justice and wise government. He is the sole kadi in his kingdom and the people are so contented that there is never friction between them and their ruler. Indeed he is worthy of your friendship, O king!"

"What you have told me and the letter which I have just read," returned the khalifat, "prove to me that the king of Serendib is a good man, filled with wisdom and worldly knowledge. Happy is the people which he governs, say I!" Then the khalifat presented me with a robe of honour and rich gifts; and, after rewarding me with privileges, commanded the cleverest scribes of his palace to write down all my story that it might be treasured among the papers of his reign.

I hastened to my own house in my own street, and lived there, surrounded by riches and respect, among my friends and relations, quite forgetting my past troubles and having no other care than to squeeze from this life all the joys of which it is capable.

Such is the story of my sixth voyage. Tomorrow, dear guests, if Allah wills, I will tell you the tale of my seventh voyage which is fuller of astonishing prodigies than the other six put together.

Then Sindbad the Sailor feasted his guests and dismissed them, giving a further hundred gold pieces to Sindbad the Porter who returned home marvelling at all he had heard.

Next morning Sindbad the Landsman made his prayer and returned, as he had been asked to do, to the palace of the other Sindbad.

When all the guests were assembled and had eaten, drunken, chatted, laughed, and listened to fair music, they ranged themselves in a silent circle around their host, who described to them:

THE SEVENTH AND LAST VOYAGE

I MUST TELL YOU, MY
dear friends, that, after my return from my sixth voyage, I put aside
all thoughts of making any further journey; for my age was beginning to be against prolonged absences and I had no longer any desire
for new adventures after the dangers which I had already run. I was
the richest man in all Baghdad and the khalifat would often send

for me to hear me tell of the strange things which I had seen during my voyages.

One day, when Haroun Al-Rachid had called me into his presence, I was on the point of beginning a recital of my travels, when he said: "Sindbad, you must carry my answer and my present to the king of Serendib; for none knows the way to his kingdom better than you and he will doubtless be delighted to see you again. Make ready to start today; for it would be little worthy of us to keep the king of that island waiting for our answer."

The world darkened before my eyes and I was in the limit of perplexity, yet I hid my feelings in order not to displease the khalifat and, although I had sworn never again to leave Baghdad, kissed the earth between his hands and told him that I was ready. He gave me ten thousand dinars for the expenses of my journey and intrusted me with a letter written in his own hand and the presents he intended for the king of Serendib. These presents were: a magnificent bed of scarlet velvet worth an enormous sum of money, two other beds of different colours, a hundred robes of Kufa and Alexandrian silk, fifty sewn in Baghdad, a vase of white carnelian dating from old time and enriched with the presentment of a bowman aiming at a lion, a pair of wonderful Arab horses and other things too numerous to mention.

I left Baghdad much against my will and embarked at Bassora on board a ship which was about to set sail. At the end of two months to a day we arrived safely at Serendib and I hastened to lay the letter and the presents before the king. Seeing me again and appreciating the courtesy of the khalifat, that kindly monarch rejoiced and wished to keep me with him for a long while; but I only consented to stay for a few days' rest and then, taking leave of him, re-embarked in my ship for Bassora, loaded with further presents.

The wind favoured us and we voyaged along pleasantly, talking among ourselves of many things; but one day, when we were a week out from the island of Sin where the merchants on board had traded, a terrible storm broke over our heads and heavy rain fell upon us. We hastened to cover our merchandise with canvas as a protection from the wet and then prayed to Allah against the dangers of our journey. While we were doing so, the captain girt up his robe and, climbing to the mast, looked for a long time to right and left. He descended very yellow about the face and, looking upon us with an expression of despair, silently beat himself about the face and snatched at his beard. We ran to him, asking what was the matter, and he answered: "Pray to Allah that He may lift us from the gulf into which we have fallen; or rather weep and say your farewells, for the current has driven us from our path and thrown us into the last seas of the world."

Then the captain opened his sea chest and took from it a linen bag, containing a powder not unlike crushed ashes. He wetted this substance with water and, after waiting a little, sniffed some of it up his nose; then he took a small book from the chest, intoned a few pages of it and then turned to us, saying: "My magic book confirms my gravest fears. That land which you see upon the horizon is the Clime of Kings, where our lord Sulayman lies buried (upon whom be prayer and peace!). Monsters and terrible serpents inhabit that coast and the sea is full of gigantic fishes, who can swallow down a whole ship at a single mouthful. Now you know the worst, so farewell!"

We remained frozen to the decks with horror, expectant of some fearful end. Suddenly the whole boat was lifted up and then cast down again among the waves, while a cry more terrible than thunder rose from the sea. The ocean boiled beside us and we saw a marine monster, as great as a mountain, plunging towards us, followed by a second greater still, and a third larger than the first two put together. This last creature leaped suddenly from the gulf of the sea, and, opening a mouth like a valley between two hills, swallowed our ship to three-quarters of its length with all that was in it. I had just time to run to the top of the slanting deck and leap thence into the sea, when the monster drew the whole vessel down into its belly and disappeared into the depths with its two companions.

I succeeded in clambering on one of the planks which had started from the ship under the monster's jaws and, after some hours of tossing to and fro, was thrown on an island covered with fruit trees and watered by a clear and pleasant river. As I wished to regain my own country, and as I saw that the river ran very fast indeed, making a noise which could be heard far off, the idea came to me to make a raft, as I had done on the island of jewels, and let myself be carried down by the current. "If I save myself in that way," I thought, "all will be for the best and I swear never again in all my life to allow the word *voyage* upon my tongue. If I perish in the attempt, still all will be for the best, as I will be quit of danger and privation for ever."

After I had eaten a little fruit, I collected a great quantity of the larger branches of a tree which I did not know, but which turned out afterwards to be sandal-wood of the very finest quality. As I had no ropes, I bound these together with the flexible stems of certain climbing plants and thus constructed a very large raft which I loaded with fruit for my journey. I embarked, crying: "If I am saved, it will be by Allah!" and had hardly pushed my craft from off the bank when it was hurried down stream at a prodigious rate so that I fell, powerless with vertigo like a drunken fowl, on to the heaps of fruit.

When I came to myself I looked about me and was dazed with a noise as of thunder; the river was one gallop of boiling foam, borne quicker than the wind, towards a yawning precipice which I heard rather than saw.

Giving myself up for lost, I clung with all my strength to the branches of the raft and, shutting my eyes so as not to see the mangling of my own body, prayed to Allah before my death. Suddenly, as I was over the very lips of the abyss, I felt the raft halted upon the water and opened my eyes to see that my craft had been caught in an immense net thrown by men from the bank. I was dragged towards the shore and lifted from the meshes of the net, more dead than alive, while my raft was pulled up upon dry land.

As I lay shivering upon the ground, an old man with a white beard advanced towards me and, giving me courteous welcome, covered me with warm garments which comforted me very much.

My strength came back under the solicitous rubbing of the old man, so that I was able to sit up, although I could not speak. My saviour supported me on his arm and led me slowly to a hammam, where I was given a bath which quite restored my spirit, and exquisite perfumes to smell and pour upon my body. Then the old man conducted me to his own house where his family rejoiced at my coming and received me in all friendship. I was seated upon a diwan in the reception hall and served with excellent food and a fresh drink of water scented with flowers. Incense was burnt about me and slaves brought warm perfumed water for my hands and napkins hemmed with silk for my beard and lips. When I was well restored by all these attentions, my host took me to a well-furnished chamber and discreetly left me alone, providing me with slaves who visited me from time to time to see that I lacked nothing.

I was entertained in this way, without being asked any questions, for three whole days, until my strength had completely returned to me and my heart become quiet; then the old man sat down beside me and greeted me courteously, saying: "O guest, may your sojourn among us be calm and pleasurable. I give thanks to Allah that He placed me upon your path to save you from the precipice. Now will you tell me who you are and whence you come?" I confounded myself with thanks to the old man for having saved my life and for his subsequent entertainment of me, and then said: "I am called Sindbad the Sailor, because of the many voyages I have made upon the sea. Those strange things which I have seen would serve as a lesson for the attentive reader even were they written with a needle upon the corner of an eye." With that I told the old man the story of my life from beginning to end, without omitting a single detail.

For a full hour he sat silent from astonishment, but at length raised his head, saying: "Now, dear guest, I advise you to sell your merchandise without further delay, for, apart from its excellent quality, it is a great rarity here."

I was astonished at these words and had no idea what they meant, since I had been cast naked among these people; yet, being unwilling to let slip any opportunity, I put on a knowing air as I answered: "That may well be." "Take no care for your goods, my child," continued my host, "you have but to come down with me to the market and I will do the rest. If a suitable bid is made we will accept it; if not we will keep your valuables in my storehouses until we can get a better price."

I did not let my perplexity appear, but answered: "O venerable uncle, whatever seems good to you is right in my eyes. After all you have done for me, I have no thought which is not yours." With that I rose and went with him to the market.

When we arrived I received the greatest surprise of my life; for there was my raft, surrounded by brokers and merchants who were respectfully examining it with many wise nods. On all sides I heard such expressions as: "Ya Allah, it is a marvellous quality of sandal! Never have we seen so fine a wood!" Then at last I understood in what my merchandise consisted, and thought it fitting to assume a proud and reserved expression.

Soon my venerable host bade the chief broker begin the auction, which he did, opening the bidding at a thousand dinars. "This raft of sandal-wood for a thousand dinars!" he cried, and my friend exclaimed: "Two thousand!" and another cried: "Three thousand!" When ten thousand was bid, the broker looked at me, saying: "There is no advance upon ten thousand." "I will not sell for that," I answered.

"My child," said the old man to me, "our market is not very prosperous just now and all goods have fallen in value. You had better accept this price, or, if you like, I will add a hundred dinars and buy the lot for ten thousand one hundred." "As Allah lives," I answered, "for you and for you alone, good uncle, I consent to sell." At once my host ordered his slaves to carry all the wood to his storehouses and conducted me back to his house, where he paid me the money agreed upon and fastened it for me in a strong locked box, thanking me all the while for my benevolence.

Later a cloth was spread for us and we ate and drank with merry conversation. When we had washed our hands, the old man said: "My child, there is a favour which I beg you to grant me." "Any tavour were easy from me to you, uncle," I answered; and he continued: "My child, I am a very old man and have no son; yet I have a beautiful young daughter who will be extremely rich when I die. If you will promise to remain with us, I will gladly marry you to this girl, and then you will be master of all I possess and all I direct in the city; you will inherit both my authority and my wealth."

I lowered my head and remained silent, so that he continued: "Do what I ask and you shall not lose by it. If you will, I modify my condition and only stipulate that you remain here during my lifetime; after my death you shall be free to take my daughter with you to your own country." "As Allah lives, venerable father," I replied, "I have no opinion other than your opinion, and am more than willing for you to direct my destiny, since every time I have tried to do so myself evil has followed. I gladly consent to this marriage."

The old man rejoiced exceedingly at my consent and sent for the kadi and witnesses, who married me to the daughter of my host. A great feast was held and at last I was conducted into the presence of my bride whose face I had not yet seen. I found her admirable both in disposition and beauty, and was delighted to discover that she wore jewels, ornaments, silks, and brocades, worth thousands and thousands of gold pieces. We learned to love each other and lived together for a long time with sport and joy.

At length my father-in-law passed into the peace and mercy of Allah and we gave him a sumptuous funeral. I inherited all his possessions; his slaves became my slaves and his goods my goods, and all the merchants of the city named me their chief in place of the dead, so that I had occasion to observe the customs and manners of the place more closely than I had done before.

One day it came to my notice that the people of the city suffered

SINDBAD THE AIRMAN

a change every year in Spring: this physical process lasted for a day and at the end of it, the men of the place had wings upon their shoulders and could fly high up into the vault of the air. During the time which this change lasted they were never out of the sky and left only their women and children in the city, because these did not grow wings. Though this circumstance was astonishing enough, I soon got used to it; but in course of time I began to feel shame to be the only wingless man in the city and to have to stay down with the women and children. I tried to find out how to grow wings on my shoulders, but my fellows either could not or would not tell me. I knew dark hours of mortification that I, Sindbad the Sailor, should not be known also as Sindbad the Airman.

One day I took aside a certain merchant whom I had helped in different ways and begged him to allow me to cling to him when he next went aloft and thus experience a new kind of voyage. At first the man would not listen to me, but at length I cajoled him into consenting and, after joyfully telling my wife what I was about to do, took tight hold of his waist and was carried into the air by the oarage of his wings.

At first and for a long time we went straight up and mounted so high that I could hear the angels singing their holy songs under the vault of heaven. This wonderful music roused so great a religious emotion in me that I cried: "Praise be to Allah in the deep of the skies! Let all creatures glorify and adore him!"

Hardly had I pronounced these words when the winged man fell through the air like a thunderbolt, with a frightful curse, and descended so rapidly that I fainted away. I should infallibly have been dashed to pieces if we had not fallen upon the top of a mountain, where my carrier left me, with a devilish glance, and disappeared in the air upon his wings. Left alone upon this deserted peak, I knew not what to do nor how to return to my wife; therefore I cried: "There is no might nor power save in Allah! Each time I escape from one misfortune, I stumble upon a greater. Surely I deserve all that happens to me!" I sat down sadly upon a rock, trying to think of some escape from my present dilemma, when I saw two young boys approaching me, whose beauty was more than human. Each held a wand of red gold in his hand and leaned upon it as he walked.

I rose to my feet with alacrity and, walking towards them, wished them peace. They answered my greeting kindly so that I was encouraged to continue: "The blessings of Allah be upon you, O marvellous youths! Tell me who you are and what you are doing." "We are lovers of the true God," they answered and then, without further words, one of them pointed out a certain direction to me and, leaving me his gold wand, disappeared hand in hand with his companion.

I took the wand and began walking in the way which had been shown to me, thinking all the time of the surpassing beauty of my guides. Suddenly, on turning the corner of a rock, I saw a gigantic serpent holding in its mouth a man, of whom it had already swallowed three-quarters. The victim's head cried out to me: "O passer-by, save me from the maw of this serpent, and you shall never repent of your goodness!" I ran up behind the snake and dealt him so well aimed a blow with the red gold wand that he lay dead upon the ground. Then I stretched forth my hand and helped the man out of the belly which had swallowed him.

Looking closely at the man I had rescued, I recognised him for the flyer who had so nearly dashed me to pieces by hurling himself from the vault of the sky to the top of the mountain. Unwilling to

bear malice, I said gently: "Is it thus that friends behave to friends?"
"First I must thank you for saving me," he answered, "and then I
will tell you something which you do not know. My fall from the
sky was occasioned by your unfortunate mention of the Name. The
Name has that effect upon all of us and we never speak it." "Do not
blame me for my perfectly innocent words," I answered, "I promise
not to mention the Name if only you will consent to take me back
to my own house." Without answering, the flyer took me upon his
back and in the twinkling of an eye set me down upon the terrace
of my own house.

When my wife saw me again after so long an absence, she thanked
Allah for my safety, and then said: "We must no longer dwell
among these people, for they are the brothers of devils." "How
then did your father live with them?" I asked; and she answered:
"My father was not of them; he did not behave as they behave, and
he did not lead their life. As he is dead, I suggest that we should
leave this wicked city after selling such property and houses as we
have in it.

"You will gain much money, so that we can buy fair merchandise
and depart to see your family and friends in Baghdad, where we can
live in peace, safety, and submission to Allah."

Using all the ability which experience had given me, I sold my
property bit by bit and realised a hundred for one on each gold
piece which the things had cost my dead father-in-law. I bought
merchandise and, hiring a vessel for myself and my wife, made a
good trading voyage to Bassora. Thence we went up stream and soon
entered Baghdad, the City of Peace.

At once I took my wife with me to my own house in my own
street, where we were both received with cordial expressions of joy.

I put my affairs in order, distributed my remaining merchandise among various shops, and could at last sit down calmly to receive the congratulations of my friends; they informed me that this last and longest of my voyages had kept me away from home for twenty-seven years. I told all those who gathered round me the story of my adventures and vowed that I would never leave Baghdad again; an oath which, as you may see for yourselves, I have scrupulously kept. You must not think that I omitted to give long thanks to Allah for having saved me from so many and so great dangers, in spite of the numerous occasions on which I had tempted providence, and brought me back to my family and friends.

Such, dear guests, was my seventh and last voyage, which definitely cured me of any further desire for travel.

When Sindbad the Sailor had finished his tale, amid a hushed and attentive audience, he turned to Sindbad the Porter, saying: "Now, my friend, consider the labours which I have accomplished and the difficulties which I have overcome, and tell me if your estate of porter has not made for a more tranquil life than that which Destiny reserved for me. It is true that you have remained poor while I have become fabulously rich, but has not each of us been rewarded according to his efforts?" Sindbad the Porter kissed his host's hands, saying: "As Allah is with you, my master, excuse the ill-timed inconsequence of my song!"

Sindbad the Sailor gave a feast to his guests which lasted thirty nights and then appointed Sindbad the Porter to be his major-domo, so that the two lived together in perfect friendship and joy.